HER FATHE

"Can't you 'ear their paddles chunkin' from Rangoon to Mandalay?

On the road to Mandalay,

Where the flyin'-fishes play,

An' the dawn comes up like thunder outer China 'crost the Bay!"

(Excerpt from Mandalay by Rudyard Kipling 1890)

BELINDA ROSE BOND

First paperback edition March 2022

Cover design by
Jenn Garside Illustration and Graphic Design

ISBN 978-1-7398603-0-1(paperback)

www.belindarosebond.com

Rose and Iris

whose strength and love

inspired me to follow my dream.

Neil,

my children,

my grandchildren,

family and friends.

Thank you.

1

All That Glitters

He was a handsome man with rugged looks, wild black hair and dark, mysterious eyes. Many women had fallen under his spell; the few that hadn't succumbed to his charms became his enemies. His name was William D'Souza: a young man from Rangoon, burning with ambition and big dreams.

Life was becoming increasingly difficult for William, and he faced the harsh reality of poverty every day. His parents had died a year previously, leaving him alone to fend for himself. Money was tight, the only work he could find being bit jobs at the market, and unfortunately, he was just one of many seeking employment and desperate for a better life.

Every morning at sunrise, he headed to the market, looking for work. Some days he managed on handouts, other days he earned a wage. It was about survival.

Many traders had known William since he was a child and we're happy to help him. He would fetch and carry stock to and from their stalls.

One morning, while laden with two large sacks of rice balanced on his back, his view diverted to the ground, he noticed an open newspaper on the side of the road. A large advertisement was spread across the page, asking for port workers. William dropped the sacks onto the ground and picked up the paper.

He read: The Commissioner of the port was advertising for workers, the article went on to explain, the ever-increasing trade was mainly due to the opening of the Suez canal several years early, which had made Rangoon an important trading port for Asia.

Was this William's big break? Offloading his heavy cargo, he quickly headed down to the port.

He was a poor man with many ambitions, one of which was to become a Wharf Manager. He imagined himself wearing the suit, the white shirt and the starched collar, and had spent many sleepless nights imagining all the trappings such a position would bring him. Lying on a cold, dusty floor with only a thin sheet for cover, he needed dreams to spur him on to a better life; they were all he possessed.

He was offered a job and, within the week, became one more port worker amongst the hundreds already employed. His day began very differently from the others, however: a Red-vented bulbul bird woke him. William had saved the bird from the claws of the neighbourhood cat, its wing was broken and it would have been easy pickings for the feline. Instead, he had cared for the tiny bird by keeping it in a small box filled with straw and fed it insects every day. Once fully recovered, Red, as he was now named, was happy to sit on William's window ledge and sing a morning wake-up call.

Now William had full employment and ate regularly, there would be no more handouts for him, and with breakfast on his mind he set out on the short journey to work, taking him past the market traders who were all busily setting up their stalls in the town square.

Farmers from all around the region were selling fresh green cabbages, racks of bananas and piles of watermelons, all carefully stacked. Women dressed in traditional long skirts were carrying bamboo baskets overflowing with pink, yellow and orange chrysanthemums. There was a beautiful array of colours – magentas, whites and yellows – and cascades of roses flowed over the stalls, awakening every sense with their display, gently enticing customers with their exquisite perfume. Coconuts in their green pods were piled high on rickety wooden tables, and rows of fresh fish ready to buy lay on a carpet of banana leaves. Shrimps, crabs, catfish and salmon with silver scales shimmering in the early morning sun caught William's eye with their sumptuous display. As he turned the corner, the delicious aroma of lemongrass, turmeric and fish broth wafted through the air towards him. Relieved to have some rupees in his pocket, he was happy to hand over the money in exchange for a delicious steaming bowl of mohinga. As he sat and ate his one meal of the day, the market square was coming to life around him; families on bicycles and rickshaws were all beginning their day.

William was used to the organised chaos and had learnt how to navigate the streets from a very early age.

Now that William was employed, he had become a small cog in the giant wheel of British business, eager for a stake in Burma's prosperity. Rangoon had seen three Anglo-Burmese wars and survived them all, and he prayed for peace and a halt to the unrest in his beautiful Rangoon. The back-breaking work in the sweltering heat and high humidity only fuelled his drive for a better life.

After yet another exhausting shift, he stopped for a few moments; the sun was setting over the landscape, the air still warm from the day's intense heat. Smooth brushstrokes of warm reds swept across the early evening sky. He watched on as the glorious spectacle unfolded before him, with the slow descent of an iridescent sun marking the end of his working day.

Determined to change his life for the better and to have his fair share, he would have to work extra hard, and although his wage was meagre now, he knew it was just the beginning. It allowed him a little cash for his favourite pastimes: women and gambling and liquor.

Whisky was his drink – it was his way to relax, allowing himself a few moments of peace from a mind that never rested. After several glasses, however, melancholy would set in, and childhood memories of a simpler life would flood his mind. He missed his parents greatly; they were gentle people who adored their only son. But as he grew older, their faces began to fade, becoming nothing more than a distant memory, a past life, replaced by loneliness, poverty and endless days of struggle.

Now his life had turned a corner: he could eat regularly and keep a roof over his head. The hardship he had previously endured had lit a fire within him, and he vowed never to go hungry again. His confidence was growing too, but so were the risks he was taking.

There was never a shortage of willing females, all wanting to spend time with William. His hypnotic charm and boyish good looks attracted them. Whether the women were married or not wasn't his concern, he just needed passion in his life and enjoyed the company of women.

Breathing in the early evening air, William watched as day turned to night over his beloved Rangoon. Nature performed its nightly ritual, transforming the sky from red to black. Small bright glimpses of a time far, far away were scattered throughout the heavens. Continuing his walk along the port side, he could see the last elephants in the distance wading through the thick black mud and lifting logs from the laung-zat onto the port side. Taking in a deep breath of the warm evening air, he walked towards the elephant's enclosure where, as he approached, he could see his favourite, Rajan, waiting with his keeper Chai. This magnificent Asian elephant stood nine feet tall, his skin dark and rough to the touch except for three small patches of pale pink on the tips of his ears.

What a handsome creature you are! he thought.

Rajan was very clever, managing to wrap his trunk around William's waist and pushing the tip into his jacket pocket.

'Clever boy,' laughed William, as he watched the apple being deftly removed and placed into the elephant's large waiting mouth. He patted Rajan's side with affection, said goodnight to them both and watched Chai lead him away for a good night's rest.

He decided to stop at his favourite place by the lake on his journey home. Sitting down on the grass, he lit a cigarette, happy for the silence after a day of unimaginable noise on the port side. Looking up at the stars, he wished for his dreams to become reality soon.

In the distance, The Shwedagon Pagoda was glistening in all its glory, standing tall over Rangoon. For centuries it had been lavishly layered with gold leaf by millions of devotees, all paying their respects and searching for answers to their prayers.

The pagoda had become a constant reminder of a higher being for William and had given hope to millions of others on their journey to a more fulfilled existence. It was a view to behold – one he would never tire of. His eye followed its ornate beauty upwards, passing the terraces, the bell, golden turban, alms bowl, lotus petals, and the banana bud. Higher and higher, it soared to the umbrella crown adorned with thousands of diamonds and rubies, all glinting in the night sky. Finally, outstretched to the stars, the magnificent diamond bud glistened majestically in the moonlight.

Breathing in its beauty, William gradually felt a calmness wash over him, reminding him that he was a mere grain of sand, a speck of dust in the universe.

He remembered back to the freedom of his childhood, of long, hot days running through the lush green jungles with his friends. So he was saddened to see so much of the landscape destroyed, flattened and cleared, making way for the new sprawling metropolis planned by the

British. Their greed was insatiable, and William was angered by what he saw.

At least the hills in the North are safe for the moment, he thought, *and Rangoon still holds tight onto her lowlands, where the small rivers and creeks make the same journey as they have always done, down to the sea.*

William's childhood memories of the green and fertile land were just that: a memory, and one that was fading fast.

Standing up from his resting place, he took a long wistful look around, then walked back towards the town, where it wasn't long before he was in the midst of chaos again. He thrived on the fast pace, pavements heaving with shoppers, families, workers and traders, all trying to get somewhere else. Market stalls were open day and night, selling their wares of fruit, flowers, vegetables, meats and fish, piled high. Makeshift lights attached haphazardly to wooden posts, enabling the street food vendors to prepare their delights. Cooks threw fresh ingredients into hot steaming woks, releasing a heady aroma of garlic, fish and chillies, mixed with the sweet smell of jasmine rice that filled the evening air.

2

Candle in the Window

William had walked the same route from the port, through the night market, for the past fourteen years; not much had changed apart from an increase in traffic and noise. There were always plenty of beautiful women for him to admire, but this particular evening was different. William tried hard not to stare but couldn't help himself. The most beautiful girl he had ever seen stood beside the flower stall, her long, silky black hair flowing behind her. She must have sensed that someone was watching her, and as she turned towards her admirer their eyes met. He had never seen anyone quite so stunning; she took his breath away. Quickly crossing the road whilst dodging the waves of traffic, he eventually reached the other side. Desperate to make the girl's acquaintance, he went to the flower stall where she had been standing, but she was nowhere to be seen; she had vanished.

Determined to find the girl again, William walked the same route for weeks until, finally, he caught sight of her again and, not wanting to lose her this time, went straight over and struck up a conversation. To mark the beginning of their relationship, William arranged a secret rendezvous for that same evening.

Isobel was a young, naive girl who hadn't experienced much in the way of life's pleasures, and William was more than happy to teach her all he knew. She had allowed him just a few embraces – and then only if she was feeling courageous. She was obviously attracted to him: what red-blooded woman wouldn't be? But she was also curious to know more about him. When she inquired about his personal life, he quickly answered that he had to care for his elderly grandmother – and hoped this would quash any further questions or curiosity.

William was determined to stop anyone spoiling his fun and so he brought forward his plan to acquire a room, allowing more time with Isobel. He wasn't worried about the situation; having been here several times before, he knew what he was doing. Her family was the only obstacle that stood in his way and he needed to get Isobel as far away from them as possible, just in case, they changed her mind.

Having arranged to meet on one particular evening, and after navigating the busy streets, he finally reached their secret meeting spot, just behind the market stalls. He knew it wasn't the most salubrious of places, but it was dark, private, and away from prying eyes. Leaning against the wooden post, William lit a cigarette and waited for Isobel to arrive. After a few minutes, he saw a hurried figure coming down the path.

As she came closer, he managed to slip his arm around her waist and pull her close to him, impatient for a kiss.

He held her close to his body, smelling her fragrant hair, and felt her slim frame against his. Then, sensing her hesitancy, he pulled away, cupped her face in his hands and gently kissed her tear-stained face.

Explaining the events of her day whilst holding back her tears, she told him that her parents had found out about their relationship and had forbidden her to ever see him again. In the heat of the moment she had raised her voice to them, saying, 'If I can't see him, I can't live here anymore.' This bold statement had left her no choice but to leave.

'But of course, now I have nowhere to live!' she wept, looking down at the suitcase by her feet.

'Please don't cry, you know I will look after you, don't you? A friend of mine has a room to rent, and it just so happens to be available today!'

'Oh, William, thank you so much! I knew I could rely on you.'

Picking up the case, Isobel followed him through the busy marketplace, walking a few steps behind as they did not want to draw attention to themselves. Once in York Road and away from prying eyes, William took her hand, passed several shops, and turned into a dimly lit courtyard. He pointed to the right, and Isobel looked up at the building.

'It's the room with the wooden shutters,' he told her.

William walked up the metal staircase attached to the side of the building, she followed. Opening the door, he spotted a candle on the table by the window and, taking a box of matches from his pocket, lit it and placed it in the holder.

The space became illuminated as Isobel entered the room, and she immediately noticed the peeling paint on the walls and a large damp patch on the ceiling above the window. The room was small and dark, a single bed was pushed into the corner with a wooden cupboard beside it and the worn, tiled floor was covered partially by a sizeable tattered rug. William watched her reaction and clearly saw that it wasn't quite what she had expected. He quickly explained how lucky they were to have found any accommodation at such short notice and reassured her it would only be temporary, just until he could find an alternative.

The condition of the room had shocked Isobel, but with William's kind words and promises she began to relax. For William, the situation was perfect: cheap rent, discreet location and far away enough from meddling parents. He was feeling very pleased with himself.

She placed the small case onto the bed, looking around her new home and then back to William.

'Don't worry, my darling girl, we will soon have this place looking like a palace. Now try and get some sleep, lock the door after me, and I'll see you tomorrow.' He then kissed her and swiftly left the room.

Listening to his footsteps quickly disappearing down the metal staircase, Isobel locked the door, went across to the bed and opened her suitcase. Knowing her fate was in William's hands had made her feel slightly nervous, but she was comforted at least by the fact that he was looking after her. After all, he had found her accommodation so quickly.

What a difference a few hours can make, she thought, as she sat down on the bed, reflecting on the day.

To think it had only been a few hours previously that she had been arguing with her mother about William. They had both raised their voices, and she could see the hurt and sadness on her mother's face as Isobel shouted those damning words: 'I am leaving home, Mother – and I will not return.'

As the house fell silent, she had walked to her room and gently closed the door behind her. Kneeling on the rug, she pulled a suitcase out from under the bed, took the small framed picture of her grandmother off the shelf and placed it carefully in the case. Then, picking up the music box from the dressing table, she turned the key and waited for the familiar music to begin. As she watched the tiny ballerina pirouetting slowly, she had been transported back to her grandmother's house: she saw herself sitting at the scrubbed kitchen table and smelt the familiar aroma of coconut, breathing in deeply. A large plate of her favourite coconut puffs had been made just for her, and placed on the table. It was her tenth birthday, and she was tearing a present open whilst her grandmother looked on, smiling.

The music stopped, and a tear rolled down Isobel's cheek, falling onto the tiny dancer. She knew there was no going back, and she waited patiently for nightfall. Once evening arrived, she opened the door and listened for voices, but the house was silent. So she tiptoed out through the front door, closing it quietly behind her, and ran to meet William.

So much had happened in twenty-four hours, ending with her in a place she didn't know. Although Isobel did not want to appear ungrateful, she *was* alone. Whilst looking at the small collection of items on the bed, she suddenly realised how little she possessed. She tried hard to convince herself that her decision was the right one but knew it no longer mattered: it was too late if it was wrong. Kneeling beside her bed, she began to pray for courage and strength to get her through the next chapter in her life. She waited in silence, and then waited some more, but there were no flashes of light, no guardian angels to guide her, only silent darkness surrounding her. Finally, taking full responsibility for the situation, she had to deal with the consequences: she was alone and quite aware that the reason she was alone was her fault.

She closed the shutters, slipped on her nightdress and placed her treasured items on the small table by the window. As she lay there, she heard distant sounds coming from the market and began to paint a picture of crowds milling about the stalls, families eating together, and the street food traders cooking delicious meals. Sadly for Isobel, her reality was very different. Leaning over, she blew out the candle, pulled the thin sheet over her body and quietly cried herself to sleep.

Several months had passed, and Isobel was slowly adapting to her new life, but the black cloud of isolation from her family continued to stand over her. The long silence between herself and her parents was painful, and she needed to have at least one person in her life who cared about her. William was that person. Loneliness was her burden to endure if their relationship continued, although when William visited, the pain disappeared and her heart would leap with joy. He would make passionate love to her, and she willingly gave herself to him. Time stood still for those pure moments of pleasure, and Isobel hoped and prayed they would never end.

Her life now revolved around William and his schedule: though some weeks she spent every day alone, other weeks he would visit several times. He planned nothing, so she just had to wait and listen for the sound of his footsteps on the metal staircase. William had asked her to place a candle in the window if she wanted him to come and see her; it had become their signal.

One evening, after a hard day at the port, William decided to visit Isobel and, as he entered the courtyard, he looked up at her room and saw the tiny flicker of candlelight in the darkness. Throwing his cigarette on the dusty ground, he stubbed it out with his shoe. He slowly climbed the iron steps, and as he opened the door, he soon realised Isobel was asleep. He blew out the candle and undressed quietly, though she stirred, opened her eyes and welcomed him into her bed.

William held her close, feeling her smooth skin and warm, soft breasts against his chest. He kissed her hard and long, and their night of passion began.

After their lovemaking, they lay on the bed, their bodies still entwined, their breath rising and falling from passionate embraces, slowing only as time passed. Moonlight flooded the room with a blue haze, and leaning over his glistening chest, still wet with beads of sweat, Isobel opened the window, allowing the cooler night breeze to flow over their exhausted bodies. William fell to sleep first, and as she watched him in his slumber, her eyes followed his strong jawline to his beautiful mouth. Her fingers ran lightly across his broad chest, as it slowly rose and fell with each breath, and his strong muscular arms – one around her waist, the other across her breast. Whilst gently stroking his handsome face, she thought how lucky she was to find such a man. Their passionate lovemaking was a new and exciting experience for a seventeen-year-old girl, and she was beginning to fall in love with him.

'When will we be able to tell everyone we are in love?' she whispered.

William stirred and answered, 'My sweet Isobel, when the time is right – and only then – can we tell everyone that we are a couple. You *are* happy, aren't you?'

'I am, it's just …,' she hesitated, '… I would like us to be married one day and perhaps have children.' She looked lovingly at William, her sweet face the picture of innocence.

'One day at a time, Isobel, what's the rush? We have all the time in the world; this is our little love nest, after all. It's our little secret. We don't want anyone to come and spoil it for us – you do understand, don't you?'

'Of course, William. I love our little nest, I was just dreaming,' and with those words still on her tongue, she drifted off into a beautiful dream, nestled in his strong arms.

William was now wide awake. His thoughts were not of marriage or children. Instead, he felt immensely proud of the skills he had taught Isobel; she had become an excellent student under his guidance. Admiring her beautiful face, he smiled to himself and drifted off to sleep.

As the sun rose above the courtyard, the cockerel crowed his morning call, waking William abruptly. Sitting bolt upright, he scanned the room for Isobel and saw her in the corner of the room, busy making tea.

'Why didn't you wake me? I have to go!' he shouted, making her jolt and spill the water.

'You were sleeping so peacefully I didn't want to wake you. I didn't think ...'

Cutting her words dead, 'No, you didn't think, Isobel, you never do!'

Isobel was shocked by his aggressive tone: he had never spoken to her in that way before. She stood silently, watching him dress and, as he laced his shoes, he raised his voice to her again.

'I have to get home to my grandmother; she will be awake now and will want to know where I am!'

'I am so sorry, William, I am!' she cried, as he walked towards the door. 'When will I see you again?' she implored, her head bowed with tear-filled eyes.

'I don't know!' he responded harshly, slamming the door behind him. Isobel rushed over to the window, flinging open the shutters, to catch a glimpse of him as he left the courtyard. Slumped on the bed, she wept.

What had she done that was so wrong? She had never seen him so angry, and she was frightened.

Night after night, she lit the candle and placed it carefully by the window, praying that he would see it and come back to her. Night after night, she lay in her bed, motionless, desperately wishing to hear the sound of his footsteps rushing up the staircase to her door. But the only sound was that of her tears falling on the pillow.

3

To Have and To Hold

William left Isobel's in a rage that morning. He slammed the door behind him and rushed down the stairs, making his way through the market.

'How could she have been so stupid, letting me sleep in?' he said to himself, angrily.

He knew he had to get home, and fast, before too many questions were asked. He didn't have time to stop; all he could think about now was getting back to Halpin Road.

After several minutes of running, he finally arrived at the front door and, trying to catch his breath as he entered the house, he shouted, 'Hello?'

'Morning, my love.' A gentle, soft voice drifted from the bedroom as William entered.

'How was your shift? I was starting to worry that there might have been some trouble.'

'Trouble? What sort of trouble?'

'It's just that you are always on time, that's all. Come back to bed if you want?' the woman said, pulling the bedsheet across to let him in.

'Let me get cleaned up first,' he replied, walking back into the kitchen. While he washed, he started to regret speaking so harshly to Isobel; he would have to make it up to her, somehow. Walking back into the bedroom, it wasn't long before he was in his wife's embrace, kissing her gently and feeling her warm, familiar body. They kissed again and gently made love with a softness that suited Catherine. She was an easy choice for William: he relaxed with her and was safe in knowing that she would always belong to him, no matter what happened.

The house they lived in was small and cramped; the only advantage of living there was its proximity to Rangoon's port, where William worked. It had been built by the British specifically for port workers. It consisted of two rooms: the front for cooking, washing and eating, and the backroom for sleeping.

As far as William was concerned, this situation was just a temporary measure. He had merely put on hold his dreams and aspirations of living in a large house with a beautiful garden – for the moment. Life was tough, and money was tight, but William never gave up on his big plans for the future; he just had to bide his time and be patient. As for Catherine, she always said she was happy and content with her life, and as she lay in his arms she wished William a happy anniversary. He had forgotten until now, of course, but he wished her the same.

As they lay there, reminiscing about the last fourteen years of their happy marriage, Catherine told him again that he was the love of her life and all she ever needed.

Catherine had been only nineteen, and William twenty-one, when they first met. She was a pretty girl, pure and innocent, and he was a fortunate man to be her first boyfriend. Her father had warned William to treat her with respect, after hearing a few worrying stories about him. They courted for a year, always with chaperones, and then married.

It had been a wonderful day. Catherine's parents had planned everything, and the ceremony took place at St Mary's Cathedral. Catherine loved her dress and had felt like a princess. She recalled William's reaction, as she walked down the aisle on her father's arm; he rarely showed emotion, but she had noticed a tear in his eye as he read his vows in front of the priest and family.

'Do you remember, William? It was a beautiful day, wasn't it?' she asked, looking up at him as they lay in each other's arms.

'Yes, it was a lovely day,' he replied.

William had always known Catherine was too good for him, and yet he demanded so much from her. He was a selfish man with many needs: the thrill of the chase, adrenaline-driven passion, the touch of a woman's body next to his. He loved Catherine, but she wasn't the woman to fulfil these. She was his wife, not his whore.

Finally, when it was time to get up, William gently moved Catherine's head from his chest, kissed her forehead and prepared himself for the day shift at the port.

Catherine woke not long after William had left, and soon began her chores. She always planned her week: Monday was washing day, Tuesday was cleaning, and every day was a cooking day. So starting her tasks at half-past six was quite normal for Catherine. She liked to prepare breakfast fresh and on the table, ready for William's return after his night shift. He would always kiss her on the cheek and immediately go and wash, saying the night shift was dirty work and he had to remove the smell. He would then sit down at the table and tuck into the large bowl of mohinga that Catherine had prepared. He was always so hungry; it made her think, *how hard must he have worked to build up such an appetite?*

Catherine recalled her mother telling her, 'Always feed your man Catherine; the way to his heart is through his stomach.'

So, heeding her mother's advice, she was happy to cater to her husband's every need, like the good wife that she was.

Every morning, the sweet aromas of ginger and lemongrass together with fresh fish would fill her tiny kitchen, not forgetting the freshly boiled egg, sliced and placed on top of his noodles, just how he liked it. But, after a few years of marriage, Catherine had soon come to realise that William wasn't perfect after all. His temper was a little short at times, and he could quickly lose it, mainly where money was concerned.

He kept a tight hold on their finances and Catherine, not wanting to get him cross, allowed him the control and was simply happy to receive her housekeeping money every Friday morning.

Times were hard, and they both knew the importance of every rupee. So, deciding to help their situation, Catherine began to take in washing from her neighbour and the surrounding houses; though it was a considerable amount of extra work for her, she was happy to do it. Initially, Catherine didn't want to take the full payment, especially from her elderly neighbour, but after the woman insisted by pushing the notes into her palm, she accepted it graciously and thanked her. William would have been furious if Catherine hadn't taken the money. She could hear him saying, 'We are poor people on a poor wage Catherine, take the money!'

Catherine knew they were poor and lived a simple life, but she didn't need much, as long as she had William by her side. Occasionally, he would show his softer side and buy her small gifts on his way back from work. On one such occasion, he entered the kitchen with a grease-covered machine in his hands and promptly placed it on the kitchen table, saying, 'If you can get it working, it's yours.'

'Goodness, William, wherever did you find this? It's filthy!'

'Do you want it or not?' he asked impatiently.

'Yes, I will see what I can do with it thank you, William.'

It wasn't long before the machine was dismantled, and she methodically laid each part of it onto a sheet of newspaper. *Now, where do I start?* she thought, rolling up her sleeves.

As a child, Catherine had spent many happy hours with her father at his business and watched as he disassembled many sewing machines, trying to find their fault. Remembering back, she cleaned every piece, just as he had done, and then reassembled. Once completed, all that was left to do was a good polish. Gold writing began to appear from under the black grease, and soon the machine looked like new. Placing it on the table, she planned to use it to make some extra money and start her own sewing business. She would begin small at first with children's clothes, there were always plenty of children in the neighbourhood, and they all needed to be clothed.

Every morning, Catherine would turn the little makeshift sign from closed to open in her front window and wait for the knock at the door. It wasn't long before a steady stream of women came asking her to make clothes for their little ones. The children formed an orderly queue from Catherine's front gate and onto the street. As she knelt to take their measurements, the children would begin to wriggle, and Catherine would tickle them under their arms; she loved to hear their laughter.

Her business was getting busier by the day, but the stacks of fabric were depleting fast, so a trip to Ava's fabric shop was definitely in order. Remembering her last visit, she could still picture the eclectic mix of fabrics and haberdashery. Hundreds of rolls adorned the shop, in every colour and design you could imagine: floral, striped, cotton, velvets and silks, all neatly laid on the wooden shelves like coloured pencils in a box. She had never seen such a vast array of material before and was so looking forward to seeing her sweet Aunt Ava again.

4

Only Love Once

Ava had been a significant influence on Catherine ever since she was a teenager. Although not an aunt in the true sense, she had nonetheless played an essential role in her life.

Catherine's father, Michael, and Ava's first husband, Phillip, had worked together in the cloth trade and become great friends. Sadly Phillip had died from a heart attack, and Ava had never quite gotten over his loss. It brought a tear to Catherine's eye thinking back to that fateful evening; she had never witnessed death at such proximity before, and the awful image had been embedded in her memory ever since.

It had been a lovely evening, shared with family and friends, as they celebrated a new contract won by Michael and Phillip.

Furniture had been moved to the sides of the room, making way for the dance floor. Wine flowed whilst the guests greeted one other. Once everyone was seated, a feast prepared by Catherine's mother earlier was brought out and placed before the guests to gasps of delight.

Catherine remembered watching Ava and Phillip dance; he had held her so close to him and swept her across the dance floor, both oblivious to their surroundings. She'd witnessed their all-consuming love and made a promise to herself – she would only marry for love – and prayed that one day, she would find someone to love her as Phillip loved Ava. He adored her and showered her with love and gifts; he was always so generous towards everyone, especially his darling wife. Every year on her birthday, he would buy her another gold bracelet; she loved them and would wear several on each arm. It had become a family joke, and if anyone asked the question, 'What shall we buy, Aunty Ava?' everyone would reply, 'Bracelets, of course!' followed by fits of laughter. *Happy times*, thought Catherine.

Thinking back to the party, she could picture everyone seated at the long dining table with crystal glasses placed meticulously for each diner. Her mother had carried in the beautiful floral centrepiece of white roses and green foliage and placed it in the centre of the table. It was stunning and, together with the overhanging crystal chandelier, added a luxurious elegance to the evening.

Once everyone was seated, Phillip stood and raised a glass to his good friend and colleague, saying, 'To my dear friend Michael – you deserve every success always – to Michael!'

Everyone pushed their chairs back, stood up and began to raise their glasses, but before they could respond to the toast, Phillip dramatically grabbed his chest in pain and slumped onto the table, smashing plates and glasses.

Her father rushed to Phillip's aid, lifting him up and gently laying him on the rug. Looking on in horror, Ava screamed hysterically at Catherine's father,

'Do something, Michael! Do something!'

The room fell silent, and everyone held their breath whilst Michael listened for a heartbeat. After what seemed an eternity, he slowly turned to Ava and said, 'I am so sorry, Ava, but Phillip is dead.'

Catherine could still remember the piercing scream; it was as though she had heard Ava's heart breaking. Running over to Phillip in disbelief, Ava had knelt beside him, grabbing him by the shoulders and shaking his lifeless body, desperate for him to come back to her. Instead, he lay silent as she laid her head on his chest, held him tightly, and screamed, 'Phillip! No! You can't leave me! You can't leave me! *I won't let you!*' Tears had streamed down her face. Catherine looked across at her father, who was in shock; she saw the colour drain from his face as her mother took his arm and helped him up.

Although she had been desperate to hold on to him for as long as possible, they had prised Ava off Phillip's body and she had then been taken upstairs, away from the dreadful scene.

Time had stood still, just for a few minutes, as they looked across at poor Phillip's body with immense sadness and Ava's distant cries could still be heard. Finally, they had called for the doctor, and the housekeeper had found a sheet to cover the body.

Catherine needed to see Ava, it had been far too long since her last visit, but her plans had always caused an argument. She only needed to mention a visit to see Ava, and William would become very defensive. One day she asked for his reason.

'I don't dislike Ava – she is a very successful businesswoman and your aunt – but I don't want her trying to get you to work in her shop. After all, she knows what a good seamstress you are. But your place is here, Catherine, you're my wife, and you have always been a very loyal one. So I don't want her to put ideas in your head. You *are* happy with your life, Catherine? You *are* happy with me? Am I not a good husband to you?'

'William, you are a perfect husband! Please try not to worry. I am just going to see Ava to buy fabric so I can make us some extra money from my sewing business. I have no intention of working in Ava's shop; I am thrilled to be at home, looking after you,' she reassured him.

Catherine was not aware of any previous arguments between William and Ava, but unbeknown to her their mutual dislike had begun on the evening of Catherine and William's engagement party, fifteen years previously.

Family and friends had been invited to Catherine's family home. Her parents had arranged a lavish engagement party for them and this gave an excellent opportunity for William to meet her family. Gliding down the large staircase as her guests looked on, she wore the beautiful, soft blue chiffon dress that her mother had chosen for her. William waited patiently, and as she reached the last step she took his hand and stepped onto the dance floor. Round and round, they glided as if they were on ice. Looking into his eyes, she knew he belonged to her now, and she was the happiest woman alive. They danced and danced till they couldn't dance anymore, and when there was a break in the music they walked to the side, both flushed and laughing.

Taking Catherine in his arms, William had almost forgotten where he was as he kissed her on the cheek, her parents looking on.

Catherine decided to get them a drink, and as William stood alone he noticed Catherine's aunt, Mrs Richards, walking towards him. He assumed she meant to talk to someone close to him since he did not know her well. To his horror, she was heading straight for him with a determined expression; to try to escape would have been futile. As she approached, she held out her hand and asked William to escort her into the garden for a spot of cooler air. He turned anxiously, in the hope of seeing Catherine, but unable to be rescued, he smiled wryly and replied, 'Of course, my pleasure.'

Once they had walked a small distance, down the steps and onto the lawn, Ava turned to face William, 'Please excuse me for asking, William, I won't go around the houses, but I need to know: how much do you love Catherine?'

Taken back by her forthright question, William replied, 'What do you mean? It's our engagement party; I am going to marry her!' He could feel anger rising from the pit of his stomach.

'That's not what I asked!' she retorted.

'With all due respect, who are you to question me? You don't even know me or anything about me,' he scorned.

'Unfortunately, I have had the great misfortune of knowing a few men just like you. Yes, I agree: I *don't* know *you*, but I know my Catherine, and she is not the girl for you. Have a look around, William. You could have any girl at this party, and you know it, so why choose her?'

'I am very fond of Catherine, of course, I love her. We are engaged to be married in a year; then we will live happily ever after. She will make us a good home, and I am sure she will be a very loyal wife. What more do you need to hear, Mrs Richards? Now, if you don't mind, I have a party to attend – you do remember it's my engagement party?'

He turned swiftly and started walking back to the house.

'I will give you money!' she shouted, trying to keep his attention.

William turned to face her, 'Money for what, Mrs Richards? Oh, I see, for our engagement! Well, that's very generous of you, I must say, and there's me thinking you didn't like me.'

He continued towards the house, and desperate for him to listen, she grabbed his arm as he passed and said, 'I will give you enough money to set up a small business of your own, but only on one condition: you break off the engagement.'

'And why would I do that, Mrs Richards? You do realise that when Michael dies, Catherine, being the only child, will inherit greatly from her father's estate, which means I will be wealthier than you? Now, I am not an accountant, but I think my loyalty must lie with my wife; thank you for your kind offer, but I will have to refuse.'

'I will be watching you, William; if you upset my Catherine, I will ...'

William stopped her. 'You will *what* exactly? If you interfere in our relationship, Mrs Richards, I will tell your precious Catherine exactly how her 'Aunty Ava' tried to sabotage her happiness. Perhaps I might tell her how you wanted me for yourself; after all, you wouldn't be the first grieving widow to throw themselves at me.'

Spotting his fiancée walking towards them, he held his arm out for Ava to take hold. Smiling at them both, Catherine said, 'I wondered where you had gone, William! I see you have met my wonderful Aunt Ava, so lovely for you two to get to know each other.'

'Yes indeed,' said William, 'We have found out that we have one thing in common.'

'And what would that be, William?' Ava asked, forcing a smile.

'That we have your best interests at heart, my darling Catherine. I am sure we can both agree on that – what do you say, Mrs Richards?'

Catherine knew nothing of William's intentions or his reasons for marrying her. She just believed he had fallen in love with her. Ava had realised William already had control over Catherine; she was infatuated with him. He played a clever game, but Ava was no pushover. She would be watching him, waiting for the day his true colours would be revealed.

5

A Stitch in Time

Several weeks had passed since William left Isobel's in a rage. All the talk of marriage and children had unsettled him, so he decided to give her a little time to miss him. But now he wanted to see her: he needed to feel her soft body against his.

As he ran up the stairs he was anticipating a warm welcome and, indeed, when he entered the room, Isobel couldn't have been happier to see him. He gave her no explanation for his absence, and she asked for none.

Sitting on the bed, William kissed her passionately, holding her close, and so another night of passion began.

As the sun rose across the courtyard, William slipped from the bed and dressed, kissing Isobel gently so as not to wake her. He then placed some money on the small table, and as the door closed, she woke and saw the pile of notes.

Knowing she needed William's money made Isobel feel uneasy. Was she a kept woman now? She had become reliant on him for money and a roof over her head. What else could she do, without a job or a family to support her? Is this what she imagined her life with him would be?

Though she loved William and had enjoyed their arrangement thus far, she now realised there *must* be more. There needed to be some changes in her life, and today was the day to start.

She brushed her long black hair, tied it into a bun and splashed her face with cold water. Then, smoothing her dress down, she checked herself in the mirror by the door. Her olive skin and deep brown eyes made her a natural beauty, though her modesty never allowed her to believe it.

Leaving the room with a new determination in her step, she walked towards the marketplace. Moving from stall to stall, she enquired whether they needed any workers, but as she continued along the long parade of shops, Isobel soon realised that looking for work wasn't as easy as she had first thought.

The sun was at its hottest, and humidity was rising; she could feel the hair sticking to the back of her neck, and her clothes were becoming damp with sweat. She decided to stop for a few minutes and shade from the intense heat of the midday sun. Casually looking through the shop windows, she noticed a small sign advertising for staff. It read: *Shopgirl required, experience preferred, please contact Mrs Ava Richards (Shop Owner).*

'Well, this could be my perfect job, and it's right under my nose! There is no time like the present.' she thought.

Straightening her dress and smoothing her hair, she turned the handle and went in. A small bell above the door rang as she entered and a well-dressed woman appeared from a back room.

Isobel noticed the woman's red lipstick; it was a shocking red, but she wore it well, and her dress looked expensive. This must be Mrs Richards, the owner, she thought.

'Can I help you?' the woman asked.

'Hello ma'am, I saw from your notice in the window, you were looking for help in your shop?'

'Yes, indeed, were you thinking for yourself?' the woman inquired.

'Yes, madam,'

'Have you any experience? Have you ever worked in a fabric shop before?'

'No, madam, I haven't worked in a shop before, but I can hand sew, and I have used a sewing machine before.' Isobel paused, before adding, 'I am a very hard worker.'

Isobel started to blush; Mrs Richards was taking a good look at her and appeared intrigued.

'How old are you?'

'Seventeen, madam,'

'Do you live with your parents?'

'No, I am an orphan; I live on my own.' She had to lie, but her blushing was becoming more apparent.

'Interesting.' Mrs Richards was now looking at her with a slightly suspicious expression.

'Come closer, girl. Do you have a name?'

'Yes, madam, my name is Isobel.'

'OK, come back tomorrow, Isobel, be here eight sharp for my decision.'

'Yes, madam, thank you.'

'See you tomorrow, eight sharp, not a minute late,' the woman shouted as Isobel left the shop.

Skipping to the staircase, she couldn't believe it: she could be working and have her own money. But, with Mrs Richards' words still ringing in her ears, to be 'not a minute late', she chose not to light the candle that evening.

As the sun rose and light streamed through her shutters, Isobel woke and gave a long stretch. She still had several hours until the interview with Mrs Richards but decided to get up anyway and make herself a strong cup of tea.

Doubts started to creep into her mind: *What if she found out about my living arrangements? Would she think badly of me? And perhaps people around the market have been gossiping about me?*

Isobel was beginning to think she wasn't good enough for the job; after all, she was only seventeen, with minimal experience of shop work or life. Perhaps Mrs Richards had the same thoughts and might be better off looking for someone else.

It was now seven thirty, and having so many questions in her head, she had convinced herself the job would not be offered to her. Why put herself through more rejection? But, on the other hand, she would never know if she didn't try.

Looking at the clock by the door, she made her mind up and decided it was now or never. Rushing to get changed, she grabbed her shoes and ran down the stairs. Standing at the shop door, she calmed herself down, took a deep breath and reached for the handle, but Mrs Richards was already there, opening the door and ushering her in.

'Well, here you are, Isobel, well done. I do insist on punctuality, it's a pet hate of mine, I can't abide staff being late. Now, shall we begin?'

Mrs Richards explained to Isobel the different types of fabrics and haberdashery, too many to remember in one day. Then she told her about the different types of customers she would serve. Next, Mrs Richard explained her duties and expectations, and Isobel began to wonder if she would remember all of the information. She kept attentive to every word and soon began to imagine working there. Isobel crossed her fingers and prayed she would get the job. She waited patiently while Mrs Richards dealt with a customer, eager to hear her decision. Walking towards her with a smile, Mrs Richards reached out her hand to Isobel, congratulating her on being successful.

'So, I am willing to give you a chance. We will arrange a trial period, initially for three months, and I will see how you get on. When can you start?'

Isobel thanked her and agreed to start the following morning at eight sharp. After settling the arrangements, she left the shop feeling like she was floating on a cloud. She could hardly believe that somebody wanted her; looking up to the sky, she thanked God for listening to her prayers.

Rising early, Isobel had to ensure she was not a minute late for Mrs Richards. As the clock struck eight, Isobel was already waiting by the shop door, ready to be taught about the stock in more detail. It was an Aladdin's cave – fabric filled every corner, an incredible array of colours: blacks to purples, pinks to reds and oranges to yellows. From cotton to velvet, muslin to satin, with buttons in every shape and colour you could imagine. Rolls and rolls of fabric stood tall along the back wall, and boxes full of tailor's chalk and pencils filled the drawers of an ornate, highly polished teak cabinet. It stood in the middle of the shop floor, with several small paper packages containing needles and tiny cardboard boxes full of brightly coloured pins piled high on the polished surface.

One particular needle was extra-long, almost half the length of her arm. Mrs Richards told Isobel the upholsterers bought them, as well as fabric, braids, thread and buttons to cover their exquisite furniture. The British dignitaries would then buy these pieces to furnish their large colonial houses. She also informed her about the tailors, many of whom were Chinese. She explained that there was a large Chinese population in Rangoon and that it was growing. Ava rubbed her hands, saying this was good news for her business. Many of them had small shops within the larger Chinese market, and they always needed quality fabrics.

Ava instructed Isobel to look after them, although she warned her they would try to haggle the price down.

'You should see some of their work, Isobel; they are so skilful and can tailor a full suit in a day. Many of their clients are British Government employees,' she announced proudly.

There was so much to remember, but that didn't dampen Isobel's enthusiasm and the days flew by. Over the following weeks, Mrs Richards watched her blossom into a confident woman who was happy to approach customers to offer help, rather than shy away from them as she had done previously. Her confidence grew, not only with her job but within herself too.

After a while, Isobel was made responsible for opening the shop for one day only.

'I think I can trust you enough, Isobel, how do you feel about that?'

'Goodness, thank you so much, madam,' she replied, thrilled to be given the opportunity.

'And by now, you can call me Ava, as we have got to know each other a little better.'

'Yes, OK, thank you, madam, I mean Ava.' Isobel was thrilled to be given this new responsibility; at last, her life was looking a lot brighter. Ava had also given her a slight pay rise to reflect her new duties. With this recent increase, she had decided to take over the payment of rent from William. It had taken quite some time to convince him, and she didn't understand his objections. Surely, if she paid her rent, it would free up money to care for his grandmother? Eventually, he agreed to the change, though somewhat reluctantly.

Using the money from her raise, Isobel decided to improve her surroundings; the old metal bed frame was still in the corner, the same broken cupboard sat against the wall in her room, and the worn wooden shutters barely covered the small window. It was time to make the room more like home. She managed to buy some paint and began the transformation. Using fabric from the shop and a borrowed sewing machine, Isobel spent her evenings sewing a new bedspread in a blue and gold fabric. *Brushing up on my sewing was a great idea*, thought Isobel, as Ava was eager for her to use her skills in the shop, and it was the least she could do to thank her for all her kindness.

Ava had brought some flowers earlier from the market to take home, and had made up a small posy for Isobel, who accepted the flowers graciously.

'You *do* have a vase, don't you?' Ava enquired. Isobel blushed, not wanting to admit she did not. 'I am sure you have one, but please take this as it matches the flowers so well.' Ava handed her a beautiful pink fluted vase.

'Well, if you're sure, Ava, thank you. I will return it once the flowers have died.'

'You keep it; I have plenty,' Ava said kindly.

Fresh flowers and a new bedspread soon transformed the room, and Isobel's first thought was to thank her mother for teaching her to sew. But then she remembered: silence stood between them, so she whispered the words onto her hand, opened the window and blew them out. As a child, her mother had taught her this. When a loved one was far away, the words would travel by the breeze into their ears.

The delicate pink vase filled with chrysanthemums, carnations and a single white rose sat in pride of place on her small table, and she began to imagine her home with William. Their house would be full of fresh flowers picked from the garden. She hoped he would notice all her hard work and admire her homemaking skills. Isobel waited in anticipation as she lit the candle at the same time every evening, its tiny glow flickering between the gaps of the wooden shutters for him to see.

6

New Beginnings

As William left for work, Catherine put on her apron and began the chores. She tried to make their home as comfortable as possible, but living in such cramped conditions was difficult.

After telling her how desperate they were for money, William had told her he would have to work the night shifts as well.

Only seeing him for a few hours between shifts was not ideal, but she knew better than to argue with him. He had made a point of telling her that every rupee counted, and if that meant working all the hours, then that was his burden to carry. Knowing this was an argument she would not win, she remained silent.

Her husband's frustration had grown; he knew deep down that there was more to life than this, and had tried to communicate to Catherine his big dream of a new home with a garden and servants, money in the bank and freedom to live a happier life without financial worries. He hated it when Catherine said the house was good enough for her, and that all she needed was him. It would make him so cross. She couldn't understand why he became so angry, but it had started to make her question

41

whether she was enough for him. He had seemed excessively preoccupied lately.

Knowing his mood would only worsen if she told him about her planned visit to Ava's, she decided to remain silent; she didn't have the strength for an argument.

Catherine wanted to look her best for the visit, as Ava always looked beautiful in her French couture. Catherine remembered listening as a teenager to Ava's stories of her travels to Paris to see the latest fashions. Her visits to the House of Worth, Salon de Vente, sounded so exciting, and Catherine dreamt of going there one day. However, as she took her favourite blue dress with the lace collar out from the wardrobe, she felt slightly disappointed; it was the only 'best' dress she owned and she hoped Ava wouldn't think it too shabby. She tried to recall the last time she had worn it, but that was so long ago that she couldn't even remember. There wasn't much call for dressing up in her life – apart from church on a Sunday, and she wore the plain grey one for that occasion. As she hung the dress back in the wardrobe, she felt sad about lying to William but excited to see her darling aunt.

Why does he always make it so difficult for me? Ava is my family; anyone would think I was going to see a man! she thought angrily.

Earlier in the month, Catherine had begun to feel unwell, and her appetite had diminished; even her favourite foods could not tempt her. The mornings were the worst part, and she struggled to get through the day or finish her chores. By lunchtime, she needed a rest on the bed. William had noticed a change in her too and had insisted she saw the doctor. Still, she kept putting it off, fearing the worst and ignoring her symptoms, until William insisted and she reluctantly booked the appointment.

It soon came around, and Catherine nervously walked to the hospital. *What will he do without me? How will he manage? I know it will be bad news; how will I tell William?*

The pungent odour of disinfectant made her feel quite nauseous on entering the building, and she waited in the corridor until they called her name.

A nurse appeared, and Catherine followed her into a room. After several questions, the nurse helped her onto the examination bed. Then, laying a blanket over Catherine's waist, she drew the curtain and remained by her side whilst the doctor examined her.

Once dressed, she sat back down, desperate for the diagnosis and with hundreds of questions flying around in her head. She watched the doctor write something on a piece of paper and tried to wait patiently.

It was no good: she couldn't wait any more. She needed to hear the bad news and prepare herself for the worst.

'Please, can you tell me now? I am ready. How ill am I, Doctor? How serious is it?'

Catherine's fingers nervously twisted a tiny lace handkerchief; she looked down, not brave enough to look him in the eye as she braced herself for the diagnosis.

Looking over his half-rimmed glasses, the doctor replied,

'Well, Mrs D'Souza, that depends on what you call ill?' Catherine felt panic wash over her, and seeing the colour drain from her face, he quickly reassured her, 'Mrs D'Souza, there is absolutely nothing to worry about; with regular monitoring from us and plenty of rest and care at home, I cannot foresee any problems.'

Catherine looked confused and frightened as he continued, 'Though you are over thirty years of age, there is no reason why you cannot go on to have a healthy baby.'

Stunned by his words, Catherine was in total disbelief. 'Baby! Did you say baby, Doctor?' she said, staring directly at him, wide-eyed.

'Yes, Mrs D'Souza, you are expecting a baby, and from my examination, I would say you are just over three months gone.'

Thanking the doctor, she left his room in a daze and walked home.

The news had come as a real shock for Catherine. Never in all her wildest dreams did she think she would hear those words, and they would certainly take a while to digest.

Catherine had prayed so hard to hear this news, and at last, after all these years, they were to become parents after all. Dropping to her knees, tears streaming down her face, she thanked God for the miracle.

The following morning, William arrived home from the night shift and, as usual, went through his routine of kissing Catherine and then going to wash and change his clothes.

Although she had struggled with sickness, she still managed to make her husband's favourite mohinga with the boiled egg sliced on top, despite stopping several times to vomit.

Once seated, William began to tuck into his breakfast as usual. After a few minutes, however, he realised Catherine had not joined him. Putting his bowl down, he looked at her with concern.

'Why aren't you eating, Catherine? Are you sick? Did you go to the doctor yesterday?' he asked anxiously, putting his head in his hands and fearing the worst.

'William, I am not ill!' she assured him.

'But you have been so pale, you're not eating, and you're tired all the time; if you're not ill, then what is wrong with you? Tell me, Catherine! You're frightening me.'

Catherine took a deep breath. 'I am expecting our child, William.'

The room went silent and Catherine's words rushed to William's ears as he stood, staring at her in disbelief. His broad arms were soon encompassing her petite body, and whilst holding her gently, he kissed her forehead, her cheeks and finally her lips. Cupping her face in his hands and struggling to find the words, he whispered, 'I will never let you down, Catherine. I will always do my best for you and our child. Thank you, Catherine, thank you.'

They embraced for what seemed a lifetime, smiling at each other, both feeling the deep joy of becoming parents.

'You are so special to me, Catherine; I love you so very much.'

'I love you too, William! At last, we will have our child, can you believe it? Thanks be to God.'

That evening, William decided that he needed to end the relationship with Isobel, especially now that he was to become a father. He had to concentrate on what was essential, Catherine and the baby must be his priority. He would have to tell her soon, but she was a young girl, she would be fine. William lied to Catherine, enabling him to visit Isobel's that evening, citing a fictitious meeting with friends.

'But what about your night shift William? We can't be wasting money, especially now the baby is coming.'

'Don't you worry. I am owed a few hours; I will go there first and explain, I'm sure they will understand in the circumstances.'

'OK, well, if you're sure it will be all right. What time will you be back?'

'Well, you know what, it might be better for me to stay at Tom's for the night. You don't want me coming home smelling of drink, especially now my beautiful wife is carrying our child,' he said, placing a hand on her stomach.

Catherine agreed and watched him as he went off to work, knowing she wouldn't see him again until the morning and then only for a short time. She could never quite understand how William managed to work nights *and* the day shifts with only a few hours' sleep. But that was her William: he was such a hard worker. She wasn't worried about him having a few drinks with his friends;

she had never seen him drunk in all their years of marriage. She was so proud of her husband, especially after hearing so many horror stories of drunken husbands who beat their wives – and worse – but not her William.

Walking to work, William thought about his loving and loyal wife. He knew she trusted him implicitly. Never questioning his whereabouts, never doubting his words, just accepting them to be true. A pang of guilt came over him when he thought back over the years of gambling, fornicating with young mistresses and drinking himself into oblivion. He had built his secret life on a mountain of lies, but now it all had to stop – he needed to change. He had a loyal wife although he knew he had never deserved her. She was far too good for him, and Ava's words were still ringing in his ears: 'If you ever hurt her ...'

7

Silent Tears

The relationship between Isobel and William had become strained, and cracks were starting to show. They both wanted, and needed, different things from the relationship.

Perhaps it was losing the excitement they had felt when everything was still fresh and new.

William had decided to go and see Isobel, even though it was late. He could see the candle was still flickering in the window as he slowly climbed the stairs. He was tired and, wondering if perhaps he shouldn't have come, he began to have second thoughts. But he knew Isobel would be so pleased to see him, so he decided to continue.

Hearing that long-awaited sound of footsteps on the metal stairs, Isobel quickly tried to make herself look seductive, dabbing a little cologne behind each ear and popping the bottle under the pillow. She stretched out naked on her side, facing the door, allowing her hair to fall casually over her breasts.

The door opened, and William entered the room. He did not appear to notice that she was naked and merely kissed her on the cheek. He undressed and climbed into bed. As Isobel laid back on the bed she was shocked by his coldness towards her. He hadn't spoken a word and she didn't know quite how to react to him. There was an emptiness in William's eyes, a look she hadn't seen before. As he laid his body on hers, he began the usual motions, which he continued until he was satisfied, and then moved away from her. Saying a brief goodnight, he turned over and within minutes was asleep.

Lying motionless on the bed, Isobel noticed a sliver of moonlight on the ceiling; it reminded her of a previous night when the room had been filled with a blue moonlit haze. She recalled how their bodies had entwined, as they held each other tight after their lovemaking.

This feels so different, she thought, as her silent tears fell; not wanting to wake him, she felt so alone. They used to talk into the early hours about everything and anything, she had loved that part of their time spent together, but tonight had not been like that at all. There had been no embraces, no long passionate kisses and no gentle caresses.

He was holding back, for some reason, and whatever was on his mind, he couldn't or wouldn't tell her.

She lay there wide awake for most of the night. Had she upset him? Perhaps that was why he behaved the way he did? He didn't want her anymore; this must be the reason for his behaviour.

It all leads to the same end, of course, she thought, suddenly feeling insignificant.

When morning came, Isobel was still awake as William stirred; he sat up and kissed her forehead. Then, picking his trousers up off the floor, he took some notes out of the pocket and placed them on the table beside the bed. She remembered how she had felt the last time but said nothing, she simply watched him dress in silence and leave.

He wasn't interested in her any more, that was clear to see. All he wanted was a woman to cater for his needs; he did not need a wife. Everything was suddenly becoming very clear. Her love for him had been so overwhelming that she never saw what was happening.

There was one thing she was sure of, though: every time he placed money on the table, every time he looked through her, she felt worthless.

Who would want me now? she asked herself. *I am a scarlet woman.*

Sitting on the edge of the bed, she bowed her head in shame at what she had become. Tears ran down her face, but she did not shed them for him. These tears belonged to her alone.

Struggling to get off the bed, Isobel forced herself to make a strong cup of tea; the clock was ticking, and she had to get ready for work. Her little job was the only positive in her life at the moment, and she didn't want to lose that too. But, if Ava found out about her relationship with an older man, would she look down on her? That would be more than Isobel could bear.

William's behaviour had helped her make the decision: she had no choice now but to gather her strength and change her life. She refused to be anybody's whore. Isobel had a hard decision to make and knew, deep in her heart, that the next time William visited would be the last.

Isobel rushed down to the shop, and as she arrived, Ava asked to speak to her in private. Isobel was worried that her boss had found out about William, and braced herself for the bad news. Thankfully, Ava was smiling as she beckoned her into the back room. Isobel followed her in and watched her put the metal pot on the stove for tea. Whilst it was boiling, Ava carried a chair and placed it next to hers, tapping the seat for Isobel to sit down. Then, she poured the tea, added a little condensed milk and handed her the delicate teacup.

'I was wondering how you were getting on in your room, Isobel? You must surely find it a little cramped at times?'

'Yes, it can be, but I have got used to it now, and I don't possess many things. It's fine, really, thank you.'

'Well, the thing is, Isobel, I do rattle about rather in that large house of mine, and I do think perhaps you need to get out of that awful room. And, on a purely selfish note, I would love to have another female for company. It gets rather lonely, and we do get on so well. You would be doing me a *great* favour,' Ava told her, clearly trying hard not to be too pushy.

'Are you asking me to come and live with you, Ava?' Isobel was shocked but also excited at this request.

'Well, yes, only if you want to. Please don't feel you have to say yes because I am your employer – it has to be entirely your own decision.'

Isobel was flattered by the offer; it would solve so many issues facing her, especially now that William was going. She began to daydream, thinking how lovely it would be to live in a proper house again with running water and soft beds, her dreams only broken by Ava's voice.

'I know it's a lot to take in. Please have a good think, you would be doing me an immense favour, but I quite understand if you chose otherwise.'

Isobel took Ava's hand and thanked her for all the kindness she had shown her. But she was only too aware of the awful mess her life had become; she needed to speak to William first.

'Would I be able to give you my decision by the end of the week? I am very grateful to you for thinking of me, but I have a few loose ends to tie up before committing. Would that be OK?'

'Of course, Isobel. Shall we say by Saturday evening, does that give you enough time?'

'Yes, and I am very grateful to you, thank you again,' Isobel replied, and leaving her cup by the side of the stove, she went back into the shop to continue her work.

Now her mind was awash with questions; she needed to talk to William, but when? Only having until Saturday evening didn't leave her much time. She then realised just how little she actually knew about him. Where did he live? Where did he work?

She prayed he would visit her this week, before Saturday, but then she remembered his last visit and wasn't looking forward to this next one.

8

A Lost Love Forever

Ava had become very fond of Isobel, and now that her offer was on the table, all she could do was wait, hope and pray that she would accept. She reminded her of her younger self with her childlike qualities, ability to love so selflessly, and naivety regarding men.

Thinking back to her past gave Ava the chills; she desperately wanted to help Isobel without seeming to interfere.

Once upon a time, she too had fallen madly in love with an older man and hung on to his every word, pretending she was so mature, though, in reality, she was just a young vulnerable girl, barely a woman. She remembered the long days of uncertainty and the many nights spent alone, crying and worrying that she might lose him. The loneliness was the worst, followed by the guilt and gut-wrenching worthlessness of being the other woman. She had been foolish enough to think that he would have chosen her over his wife. She remembered the deep shame she had felt, every time she looked at her reflection in the mirror. Thankfully, it hadn't been too long before she realised that she deserved more – and much more than he was ever likely to give her – vowing never to let herself feel so helpless and used by a man, ever again.

Ava knew what was happening in the room above her shop; she wasn't a fool. The candle in the window, the absence of family and friends and the comings and goings of a mystery man under cover of darkness meant only one thing.

Ava had asked a few associates to keep a watch on the room discreetly; they were happy to spy for her for a small fee, though it was not her intention to spy at all, more to protect. Nevertheless, after several weeks without a positive description of Isobel's visitor, it had become very frustrating. One day she would uncover his true identity and hold him accountable for his behaviour.

Becoming a woman of means had never been Ava's ambition; she would have been happy staying at home with children, but God had not blessed her with them. Instead, she had been given choices. Owning several businesses, she became a shrewd, successful businesswoman in a man's world, which was unusual and not usually tolerated. But Ava had a certain way about her that put even her most ardent rivals at ease. After many years she was now a well-respected member of the business community.

Pride in her appearance was always important to her, and she was an attractive woman with striking eyes and raven black hair that had usually worked in her favour. Ava would apply her favourite red lipstick every morning like a soldier wears his armour. She was battle-ready for the busy workday ahead. But outside of business, she had become a social recluse, only going out to work and coming straight home afterwards.

She only ever had one true love in her life, her first husband Phillip; they had shared an overwhelming, all-consuming passionate love affair from the first day they met until the day he died. Though she had married for a second time to Richard, it was for companionship, nothing more. He was a kind and thoughtful man and never demanded anything of her.

Sadly, he had also died – not a sudden, shocking death like her Phillip, but a slow, drawn-out passing. As a dutiful wife, Ava had cared for him, showing him love and compassion. Then she had found herself alone once more, so she threw herself into her work to build her empire. Ava's wealth allowed her many luxuries: a beautiful house, clothes from Paris and anything else her heart desired. But with no one to share it with, it soon became an empty vessel.

The house was too large just for her, but she could not bring herself to sell up for fear of losing the memories of her life with Phillip, ingrained in every brick. But the truth of the matter was she was lonely and longed for company, just someone to sit and drink tea with, share gossip with, or to accompany her on a shopping trip.

She rattled about at Sunbird House on her own, apart from Bo and Cheng – her housekeeper and gardener. They had saved her from herself when Phillip died, and she would be forever grateful, but they *were* 'the help'. She needed company and hoped Isobel would make her decision in Ava's favour. Saturday was getting ever closer.

9

The Demon Drink

Isobel needed to speak to William urgently; she wanted to end the relationship as soon as possible.

Getting herself ready for bed, she lit the candle and placed it by the window as usual and waited patiently, listening for the sound of his footsteps. Whilst lying in the small bed, she began to think. She had given up everyone for this man: her family, her friends. The guilt and the shame she had brought on herself and her family was almost unbearable. How could they ever forgive her? How could she ever forgive herself?

She was stopped in her thoughts by the familiar sound of footsteps coming up the metal staircase towards her room. Quickly wiping her tears away, she climbed out of bed, ready to greet William. She would not let him see her tears; she needed to be strong.

Sitting on the edge of the bed, she was ready.

The door handle turned, and William fell into the room. Isobel jumped with fright, soon realising he was drunk.

'Sorry about that,' he said, trying to stand up. 'Had a little too much to drink tonight. Now, where's my beautiful girl?'

He lunged towards Isobel, but she managed to move out of the way just in time as he landed face down on the bed.

'I'm so sorry, forgive me, my beautiful Isobel, now where are you?' He looked around the room and she froze; she had never seen William like this before.

He was attempting to sit up and, after several failed attempts, he succeeded and looked directly at her.

'Have you missed me, then? he said, slurring his words.

'Yes, of course, William.' Isobel was now starting to feel frightened; he had a menacing look in his eyes that she did not recognise. Beckoning her to sit next to him, he patted the bed and, as she reluctantly sat down, she smelled whisky and stale tobacco on his breath.

'Why have you drunk so much, William? This isn't like you.'

'Ah, well, that's for me to know,' he replied, tapping the side of his nose with his finger. 'Nothing for you to concern yourself with, my beautiful girl, now come and show me just how much you have missed me.'

Isobel knew what he was proposing, and she was frightened of him for the first time in their relationship. Her instincts were screaming at her.

Run, run, she thought, *I need to get out of here now*, but as she started to get off the bed to make her way towards the door, he grabbed her arm, pulling her back with a jolt.

'And where do you think you're going? I've only just got here!'

He was now shouting at her, and any playfulness in his voice had disappeared. He pulled her over to the bed and stood over her. Determined to fight back, she grabbed at his face, scratching him just above his eye. She regretted her action immediately; he was furious now and consequently pinned her arms down using all of his weight.

'William, get off! You're hurting me!' she screamed in fear. She had never seen this rage in his eyes before, as he whispered in her ear with the stale smell of whisky filling her nostrils.

'Ssssh! You will wake the neighbours, and we can't have that, what will they think? A lovely girl like you having men visitors in your room at night!'

Isobel froze as he climbed onto the bed, still holding her arms tightly. He straddled her, transferring his weight onto her arms so she couldn't escape. He placed one hand over her nose and mouth; the other pulled her nightdress up around her waist.

Please God, please God help me. She was now praying for her life. Unable to breathe, with his hand still pushing firmly down over her face, the other grabbing at her underwear.

Is this where I die? Is this it? Is my life over? She could feel herself beginning to drift into death. Then, just for a split second, he lifted his hand from her mouth; this was her chance to scream for help. As she took a frantic gasp of air, a forceful blow hit her face, and all went black.

'Isobel, are you in there? You are late for work!' Someone was shouting from the other side of the door. Isobel woke up and tried to get out of bed, but her whole body hurt. Then, slowly sitting up, she noticed a rip in her nightwear.

Bang, bang, went the fist on the door, becoming more frantic and louder. Still very dizzy, she pushed herself off the bed, pulled her nightdress down over her hips and shuffled past her torn underwear on the floor.

'I'm coming,' she called quietly whilst slowly making her way to the door. Clutching her stomach in pain, she passed the mirror and stopped dead. Who was this person looking back at her? A swollen face with eyes so bruised, a small patch of dry blood under her nose and a deep cut, the blood had congealed on her lower lip.

Her whole body began to shake; reaching for the door, she managed to turn the handle. The door opened to reveal Ava, who stood there ready to shout at her for being late but now looking at her in horror.

'Isobel! Oh my God! Who did this to you?'

Unable to reply, Isobel collapsed in Ava's arms.

Hearing whispering beside her, Isobel tried to open her eyes, but the pain was too great. Where was she? She wanted to cry, but no tears came; she was frightened. Then she heard a familiar voice and a soft hand touched hers. It was Ava.

'You're safe now, Isobel. You're safe,' she said.

10

Truth Will Out

Willem woke abruptly to find himself face down on a cold hard floor. Confused, he lay there for a few moments. Was he still drunk? Fumbling about in the darkness, and with only a strip of moonlight around the door, he finally managed to stand up. The room was spinning at great speed, and he lurched towards the light. Pushing the door open, he zigzagged down the metal staircase, relieved when he reached the bottom. It was pitch black outside, however, and he staggered into the darkness with his vision still blurred.

He promptly fell over a bicycle parked up at the side of the pavement. Picking himself up, he continued to shuffle along the dusty road until he saw an empty rickshaw. After pulling himself up into the cab, he immediately closed his eyes and fell back into his drunken stupor.

Several hours had passed by the time William was woken abruptly by the sound of angry shouting. He soon realised that it was morning, and the voice belonged to the rickshaw driver who was impatient to start work.

'Yes, sorry, sorry,' he apologised to the driver, whilst handing him some money. He noticed that his trouser buttons were undone, so adjusted himself before stepping out of the cab. Shading his eyes from the glaring sunlight, which wasn't helping his pounding head, he walked the slow journey home, desperately trying to piece together the events of the previous evening. His last clear memory was of leaving home to end the relationship with Isobel, but he had no recollection of having seen her. Entering a dark, smoky bar on the other side of town was one vague memory coming through the fog in his mind. He recalled meeting his friends, they had chatted, and he had announced that he was to become a father.

Oh, yes – certain parts of the evening were coming back to him. He remembered music playing in the background and several Thai waitresses wearing revealing outfits milling around in the bar. A young waitress had come over to him and sat in his lap. From his headache, he could tell that there must have been plenty of whisky flowing. He remembered seeing several shots being poured and placed on a tray, and the barman shouting to one of his girls to serve them. William had grabbed one of the waitresses, perhaps a little too harshly, and the sizeable Chinese barman had not been pleased with his behaviour. He recalled the large machete in the man's hand and the cigar in the corner of his mouth. William had soon left the bar after that. The next thing he knew, he was waking up in a tuk-tuk with its furious driver shouting in his face.

William arrived back at the house looking very messy, trying to straighten himself up as he entered the house.

He shouted, but received no reply, then noticed that the bed was made and everywhere was neat and tidy. Where was Catherine? *It's still early*, he thought, then panic set in. *Oh no, what if it's the baby? What if something is wrong and she is in the hospital?*

Frantically calling her name, he ran outside to see if she was in the courtyard behind the houses, but there was no sign of her anywhere. Running back into the house, he spotted a small note propped up against the vase on the kitchen table: *Dear William, there is plenty of mohinga in the pot, and the egg is on the side. I will be going to Ava's shop this morning to buy some fabric. I thought it would be good to start making some baby clothes for our little arrival. Love, Catherine xx P.S. I hope you had a good time last night. I look forward to hearing all about it.*

William slumped down in the chair, relieved that Catherine was all right but not happy that she was visiting that bitch, Ava. He couldn't dwell, time was running away, and he would be late for work. As he splashed his face with cold water, he winced; looking in the small mirror, he noticed a deep scratch above his eye. *That's strange*, he thought, *how did that happen?* Dismissing it as part of a drunken night, he sat down at the table and ate his breakfast while his head continued to pound. Feeling the alcohol in his veins still, he hoped the brisk walk to the port would sober him up.

Earlier that morning, Catherine had decided to visit Ava to tell her about the baby. She didn't know when

William would be back, or if he had gone straight to work, so she decided to leave him a note; he worried about her so, especially now that she was with child.

The warm sun touched her face, and she took a long, slow breath of the morning air. It felt good to leave the house. As she walked down the street, however, she noticed how much busier her neighbourhood had become. Her friends had taken in lodgers just to make ends meet and she had been told by Mrs Sharman, who lived in the corner house, that thirty Indian port workers were being crammed into those tiny houses just a few streets away.

'That can't be right!' said Catherine, picturing the awful overcrowding.

William had recounted several horror stories of the mistreatment of the immigrant port workers, and she had begged him to do something to help them, but he would always reply, 'It is what it is; what can I do?'

She tried to block it from her mind, especially now that she had happier thoughts to dwell on. Her life was too busy for gossip, her small sewing business was busier than ever, and she had plenty of new customers. Her dressmaking skills were the talk of the street, and with a constant stream of customers, the fabric pile was diminishing fast.

Her journey took her out of Halpin Road, down Budds Road, and in the distance, she could see the Shwedagon Pagoda, glimmering in the sunshine. After visiting it many times as a child, the pagoda had long been William's favourite place, and he never tired of its magnificence. He told her it helped clear his mind of work problems, not that he ever discussed them with Catherine – he always kept those sorts of issues to himself.

Catherine was always happy to spend an afternoon there with him, and although they had both been brought up strict Catholics, the draw of its beauty and peace transcended any religion.

Continuing on her walk, she saw St Mary's Cathedral on the nearby road. Whenever she passed by, if time permitted, she would go in and light a candle. She and William had been married at St Mary's fourteen years previously, and there had always been a hope that one day their children would be christened there too.

Thanks be to God, she thought, now knowing that her dream would soon become a reality.

When Catherine arrived at the busy market, it was in full flow, with traders selling their wares and customers milling about. A floral aroma filled the air, and the flower stalls were overflowing with orange, pink and white chrysanthemums and roses in every colour imaginable. It was a beautiful sight to behold. Catherine picked out a small selection of flowers to give to Ava, knowing how much she would enjoy them. The fish stall was crammed with silver carp, tilapia, catfish, shrimp and lobsters. William's favourite was shrimp, and it all looked so fresh and ready to buy that she made a mental note of what to get on the way home.

Best not to buy it yet, she thought, knowing Ava would not appreciate the smell of fish in her perfect little shop.

A sudden loud noise made Catherine jump as she turned into York Road. There was a rhythmic banging of metal on metal and, being curious, she headed towards the sound to investigate. Seeing that it was coming from a nearby shop, she remembered a story William had told her about him buying her a birthday gift of gold leaf from the goldsmith. Stopping in front of the shop, she watched the man at work; he smiled, nodded his head and continued to beat gold coins with a small hammer on his anvil until they became paper-thin. He then shouted an instruction in Urdu, and his wife appeared from the back room. She nodded to Catherine, who reciprocated with a slight bow, collected the gold leaf and handed him some more gold coins, and so it continued. Catherine thought again about the gold leaf sheets William had given to her. Why had he come all this way when there was a goldsmith so much closer to home?'

Goodness, she thought, *I must hurry, or I won't have much time to spend with Ava.*

She was so excited to be seeing her old family friend; it had been far too long since her last visit. Continuing down York Road and passing several stalls and shops on her way, she eventually arrived at Ava's haberdashery.

As she entered the shop, a bell above the door rang. Looking around the shop, she called for her friend, 'Ava?', but there was no response. Thinking she must be in the stock room, Catherine walked towards the back of the shop. 'Ava, are you in there?'

Spotting someone behind the rolls of fabric, she began to approach her but soon realised it was just the shop girl.

'Good morning, madam. Can I help you?' inquired the girl, looking at Catherine.

'Good morning. I was looking for Ava; is she about?'

'Oh, sorry madam, she is not in today.'

'Goodness, is she ill?'

Catherine knew Ava never took a day off unless it was life or death. She had always had a rigorous work ethic; it had to be a significant reason.

'No, she isn't ill. I shouldn't tell you really, please do not repeat this. If Mrs Richards found out that I have told you, she would be very cross with me, especially as this is a sensitive matter.'

Catherine was becoming increasingly concerned. 'Please tell me; Ava is an old family friend – we have known each other for many years.'

'Well,' the girl began, 'I don't know every detail, but the young girl in the room upstairs, who by the way also works for Mrs Richards, was attacked in her bed last night.

'Mrs Richards had gone up to see why she was late this morning. Anyway, she said she knocked and knocked, till the girl – I think her name is Isobel – eventually answered the door. Mrs Richards couldn't believe the sight before her, those were her exact words. As the door opened, the poor girl just collapsed into her arms. According to Mrs Richards, the girl's face was swollen and cut, and her nightdress torn, and she seemed very dazed. She managed to get the girl back onto the bed, then called for help, and now they are both at the hospital. I can leave a message for her if you like, although I am not sure when she will be back in the shop.'

Catherine was stunned on hearing such dreadful news. That *poor* girl.

'What sort of monster would behave in this way towards a young girl? I hope they find whoever did this to her and lock him up!' she replied, reeling from the image in her head.

'Yes, I agree madam, I am sure Mrs Richards has got her 'friends' looking into it,' replied the girl.

'I will contact Ava – Mrs Richards – myself,' Catherine said. 'Thank you for your help, but when she does come back, can you tell her Catherine D'Souza came by; and could you put these in water for her? Thank you.' She handed over the small posy.

'Yes, of course, madam,' the girl replied, taking the flowers before returning to her duties.

Catherine struggled to get the young girl's face, bruised and swollen, out of her head. Walking back through the market, she passed the fruit and fish stall and completely forgot to purchase any fish; she simply needed to get home. Once there, she made herself a much-needed cup of tea. Sitting down in her tiny kitchen, images of the poor girl's face were still on her mind. Deep in thought, the clock striking midday made her jump, marking the start of her afternoon chores.

William resolved to visit Isobel that evening to end their relationship. He recalled that he had every intention of seeing her the previous evening, but somehow he never made it there. Thinking back over his drunken night out, he thought, *I must have been highly intoxicated to have ended up sleeping in a rickshaw! Isobel wouldn't have let me in the room, let alone allowed me to talk to her.* He felt somewhat ashamed of his behaviour.

Walking through the market, with all its usual chaos, he found himself reminiscing about Isobel; he pictured her standing by the flower stall. But, just like the first time he saw her, she was a vision.

He *had* cared for her; she was a lovely young woman and he had very much enjoyed their secret affair. Having a beautiful and willing young woman at your beck and call was every man's dream. But this was a sacrifice he had to make, especially now Catherine was pregnant. Their arrangement had to come to an end. He knew Isobel would be fine and would probably go back to her family. Their affair would become history, a distant memory.

Crossing over the busy road, he continued down York Road and turned into the courtyard. The bright lights of the market slowly disappeared behind him. It was the same route he had taken many times before and always with heady anticipation of the night ahead. This would be his last visit to Isobel's, and he looked up for one final time for the familiar flicker of the candle – but there was none.

Undeterred by the absence of the usual signal, he climbed the metal steps and knocked on the door. Perhaps Isobel was asleep? He went to turn the handle, but the door was already ajar. Stepping into the dark room, he whispered her name so as not to startle her, but there was no reply. William found a match, struck it on the bottom of his shoe and lit the candle. Then, walking towards the bed, he gently pulled the bedcover off it, only to find it empty.

Where could she be at this time of night? And why had she left the door unlocked? *Well, wherever she is, there better be a good explanation when I see her next!*

He blew out the candle and slammed the door behind him. *What if she is out seeing other men? I have caught her out!* William began to imagine all sorts of deceitful acts she could be performing with other men, and the fire of jealousy rose from the pit of his stomach. *How could she do this to me? And after all I have done for her – the ungrateful little whore!*

With dark thoughts whirling through his head, he ran down the stairs and marched across the shady courtyard back out onto the street. Furious with rage, collided with someone, knocking them to the ground. Through the darkness, he could see the silhouette of a woman. Bending down to help her, he apologised for his haste and retrieved her case from the dusty ground. Holding it out to her, he waited whilst she brushed the dust from her dress and, as she snatched it angrily from him, she suddenly recognised him. Moving closer for a better look, she said, 'Well, well, well. William D'Souza, whatever are you doing here?'

Recognising the voice immediately, he replied, 'Good evening Ava. What are you doing here – and so late?'

'I needed to collect some things for a friend; she is in hospital.'

'Oh dear, nobody I know, I hope?'

'No, no … you wouldn't know her.' Changing the subject quickly, Ava continued, 'William, I thought you worked nights?'

'Yes, I do, but I finished earlier tonight.' William's palms were beginning to sweat.

'Why were you on the stairs?' Ava waited patiently for an answer.

'A friend of mine was looking for a room, and they told me about this one; he asked if I would have a look at it for him.'

Impressed by his own quick thinking, William thought it a good deflection from the real reason he was there. But his swift answers only made Ava more suspicious.

'Well, you can let your friend know it is not for rent. How is Catherine, by the way? Is she well?'

'She is very well, thank you.' William was by now eager to get away.

'Good, tell her I will pop and see her very soon.'

'Of course I will, Ava. I'd better be getting home, Catherine will worry. Goodbye.'

William brushed past Ava and continued to walk down York Road towards home.

Ava stood there for a few moments, shocked to have seen him there. He was a man with guilt written all over his face. She suddenly became frightened; glancing quickly to check that he had gone, she ran to the room. Her hands shook as she lit the candle. It was warm which meant he had already been there. Realising she was in the exact spot where the attack took place, she felt the panic in her rise and, grabbing the remaining items, she bundled them into the case and ran down the stairs and across the dark courtyard, her heart pounding out of her chest. Fumbling for the shop keys; once retrieved she tried desperately to open the door, but in her panic, they fell to the floor with a clang. Reaching down, the tears in her eyes obscured her view and she felt along the ground till they were found. She tried again, looking nervously over her shoulder. Once in, she bolted the door and slumped down on the floor, she had never been so frightened in all her life.

Had she just come face to face with Isobel's attacker, the monster who had raped her?

Ava had always had her suspicions about William and had never trusted him, ever since their heated discussion at the engagement party. It was all beginning to make sense to her. Hugging her knees, she bowed her head and wept.

Eventually, she stood up, steadying herself on the counter, but the thought of her darling Catherine being in the same house as that monster just made her weep even more.

11

A Cup of Kindness

How could she leave the shop? William had been caught out and he might be waiting for her. She had seen what he was capable of for herself and he showed no remorse. What else was he hiding?

Too frightened to leave the shop, she could picture his silhouette in the dark shadows and it sent an icy chill down her spine.

As the sun rose, a stream of daylight flooded the shop. Looking up, Ava realised she had been there all night. Reaching for the coffee pot, she placed it on the small stove and pulled a box close to her chair. She put her stockinged feet up on it and closed her eyes for a few minutes.

The sweet aroma of coffee filled the stockroom, and Ava woke with a start. Reaching for a cloth, she lifted the boiling pot off the stove and poured herself a well-earned coffee.

She had a busy day ahead, despite the events of the previous night, so she reached for her handbag and took out a gold compact and lipstick. Then, carefully dabbing a small powder puff across her nose and cheeks, she reapplied her red lipstick: now she was ready for the day, whatever it may bring. She needed to see Catherine and make sure she was fine, she prayed William wouldn't be there and wondered how she would be able to keep her recent discovery from her good friend.

Looking through her stockroom, she gathered several fabric remnants in various colours and filled a small basket, adding sets of buttons, a few reels of thread and two panels of lace. She hoped this small gesture would take Catherine's mind off the whole unsavoury situation in the room above the shop and, knowing how much Catherine loved to hand sew, Ava was more than happy to give her the small gift.

After writing a note for her staff, she grabbed her handbag, Catherine's basket, and Isobel's suitcase. Leaving the shop laden with bags, she headed towards the market, searching for a rickshaw. A small crowd of drivers gathered along the pavement, and one of them helped her onto the rickshaw. Once she had informed him of the address, she sat back and closed her eyes for a few minutes.

'Memsaab, Memsaab.'

'Memsaab, Memsaab.' Ava woke with a jolt, she must have nodded off for a few moments; the driver was announcing their arrival. Stepping out of the cab, she walked towards the house and was ready to knock on the door, but stopped herself.

I can't tell her, she thought, *It would break her heart and ruin her life. I cannot be responsible for that.*

Catherine had a right to know who she was married to, but today would not be that day. Would he hurt his wife? In all the years of their marriage, he had been controlling and obstinate but never violent; if he had been, Ava was convinced Catherine would have told her. Taking a deep breath she knocked and waited for Catherine to answer. The door opened after only a few moments, and Catherine stood there, surprised but delighted to see her.

'Ava, how lovely to see you! I wasn't expecting a visit, please excuse me,' she said, trying to tidy herself. 'I haven't had time to do my hair.'

'You are still my beautiful Catherine, with or without your hair done!' Ava laughed.

'Come in, come in – it's so lovely that you are here!' With great excitement, Catherine led her into the house.

'Please sit down,' she said, pulling a chair out from under the table.

Noticing the suitcase in Ava's hand, Catherine laughed and asked if she was going on a trip.

'I am sorry it's very early, Catherine, no time for a vacation, I am afraid; I have to get to the hospital to visit Isobel and have just gathered a few items from her room,' Ava replied, looking down at the small suitcase. 'Goodness knows how long she will have to stay in there. I believe my young shop girl told you all about the horrible happenings in the room above my shop?'

'Yes, she did. It's just so shocking: the poor girl! Your assistant also mentioned that she works for you too?'

'Yes, she has been with me for a few months now; such a lovely girl – reminds me of myself at that age. I will need to have a good talk with her and get to the bottom of it all. We need to find this monster before he attacks another poor girl.'

'Absolutely, he could be anywhere. Did she see who it was?'

'I haven't spoken to her about any of it yet. I managed to get her to the hospital – she looked terrible, Catherine. God only knows what that poor girl endured.'

'Try not to worry, Ava, she is young, and I am sure she will make a full recovery and hopefully will be able to put all of this frightening affair behind her.' Catherine placed a reassuring hand on Ava's.

'I do hope so. We had only just been discussing her moving to Sunbird House, and as you know, the house is so big I thought it would be good company for me. I was waiting for an answer when all this happened; she surely won't want to go back to that room? I will ask her today about coming to my house to recuperate.'

'Does she have any family? Is there anyone that you should contact?'

'I don't think so. Well, I am not sure: she told me she was an orphan.'

'Poor little lamb, she must have been so frightened.'

'Isobel may be young, but I am sure she must have put up a fight; whoever did this to her didn't go unscathed, I would say,' replied Ava. She could feel the anger building but remained calm.

'Let me make you a cup of tea. William will be back soon. It might be better not to mention what happened to that poor girl, Ava. He worries enough about me coming to you; if he knew about this, it would make it even more difficult.'

'It might be better if I go. I don't want to cause any more problems between you two on my behalf.'

'Nonsense, I won't hear of it, Ava, I'm sure Willam will be pleased to see you,' Catherine replied. Ava wasn't convinced. 'He would be horrified to know such a person is roaming the streets at this very moment, goodness, it is a frightening world, Ava.'

'Yes, it is, I am so sorry to say; we have to be vigilant. I wouldn't have mentioned it but my shop girl told me she had already discussed the whole sorry event with you. I was not very happy with her.'

'Well there is no need to worry Ava, thankfully I have William to protect me,'

As Catherine stood up to make some tea, the door opened and William walked into the kitchen. He was shocked to see Ava sitting at his table. His mind began to race. *Why is she here? What has she said to Catherine?*

He looked across at his wife and was relieved to see her in a pleasant mood. Turning to face his smiling enemy, and trying to remain calm, he said, 'Good morning Ava, this is a pleasant surprise! To what do we owe the honour of your company?'

'I missed Catherine when she visited my shop yesterday, so I thought I would visit her before I opened.'

Catherine quickly intervened, 'Yes, I tried to get some fabric, but Ava had some important business to attend to.'

William moved to Catherine's side and kissed her cheek. 'Please excuse me, ladies, but I must wash and change.' He turned to go into the backroom, just as Catherine noticed the deep scratch over his eye.

'Looks like you have been in the wars, William?' she said, pointing to the area above his eye. He raised his hand and winced as his fingers brushed the cut, which was still raw.

'And you have bruised your knuckle too, William: whatever have you been up to? Looks like there might have been an altercation?' asked Ava.

'It happened at work; it's just a cat scratch, nothing to concern yourself about,' he replied sharply.

'William, Ava was only concerned, you don't need to be quite so sharp.'

William glared at Catherine, he didn't appreciate being reprimanded like a child in front of Ava, but he also needed to avoid an argument, so quickly changed the subject.

'Catherine, have you told Ava our wonderful news yet?' he asked, deflecting the focus away from himself.

'Oh, my goodness, no! I was going to tell you yesterday but you weren't at the shop. Ava, we are going to be parents!'

Ava was shocked by the news, but she knew how much this meant to Catherine.

'I can't believe it; I am so happy for you, Catherine!'

'Well, I think you need to congratulate William as well,' said Catherine, nodding her head towards her husband.

'Of course, how silly of me. Congratulations, William,' she replied, still reeling from the news.

'Yes, we are over the moon, just think, Ava, we could have a little Catherine or a little William! Now, if you will excuse me, ladies, I have to change,' William replied, as he walked off into the bedroom.

Ava felt even more worried now, how could she tell Catherine the father of her child was the attacker? To see Catherine's face light up and see her joy was torture for Ava.

'Are you alright Ava, you have gone very pale? Here – have another cup of tea,' Catherine said, handing her a small china cup. She recognised it as one of the wedding gifts she had given to them.

'You *are* happy for us, Ava?' Catherine asked anxiously.

'Yes, of course, you have waited so long for this moment. Don't let me spoil it, just a bit of a shock, that's all.'

Ava then handed over the basket of fabrics and goodies to Catherine and saw her face light up with delight. 'I can sew some clothes for the baby; oh Ava, look at this lace!' she said, pulling the panels from the basket.

Taking Catherine's hand, Ava said, 'I am so happy for you, Catherine. May God look over you and keep you safe.'

'Thank you.'

They exchanged kisses and said their goodbyes. Ava turned and embraced Catherine, saying, 'Please remember, I am here if you need anything, anything at all.'

Climbing back into the waiting rickshaw, Ava continued to wave until she turned the corner, and Catherine watched until she disappeared from sight. She felt a slight uneasiness. Is Ava holding something back from me? she thought. She decided she was probably just imagining it, and went back into the house to see William.

The rickshaw continued in the direction of the general hospital, and on arrival, Ava dismounted and walked through the large entrance to the reception.

Equipped with the relevant information of Isobel's move to a new ward, she walked down the long, white, sterile corridors. The pungent smell of disinfectant brought back memories she would rather forget. She hated hospitals, and memories of her beloved Phillip came flooding back. As far as she was concerned, hospitals meant death, heartache and sadness. The last time she had been here was the night her husband had died. They had brought him to the mortuary, and the vision of his pale, lifeless body still haunted her. Who would have thought that, in a split second, her whole life would have changed as her loving, funny, handsome husband died in front of her, leaving her all alone? Every day she felt the pain of losing him – time was *not* a healer – and tears began to well up in her eyes. Briskly wiping them away, she told herself that today was not about her or Phillip: it was about Isobel. Pushing open the door, she walked into the ward.

A nurse showed her to a side bed near the window; the curtains were closed. She was feeling slightly apprehensive as she wondered if Isobel would even want to see her.

Gently calling her name, Ava stepped into the gap between the curtains, placed the small case on the tiled floor, and pulled the chair closer to the bed. Unfortunately, this now allowed her a perfect view of Isobel's battered face. Trying hard to hold back the tears, she reached out and took the girl's hand. Isobel turned towards Ava but said nothing, her eyes vacant of emotion. For that moment, the silence was appropriate, there were no words to describe her feelings, and there were no words that could comfort her.

An hour had passed, with still no words from Isobel, but Ava was in no hurry; she knew Isobel would eventually speak when she was ready. So she sat patiently and, after a while, saw Isobel drift off to sleep. Ava carefully slid her hand away and went in search of the doctor.

He had finished his rounds and was going back to his office, so she followed him and knocked on the door.

'Enter,' came a voice from within the room.

'Good morning Doctor, could you spare me a few minutes, please?'

The doctor looked up from his desk and recognised her. 'Good morning, it's Mrs Richards, isn't it? I was on duty the day you brought your daughter in.'

'Oh yes, hello – but she is not my daughter. She is one of my employees.' Ava was slightly taken aback by his keen observation.

'Oh, I see. Has she any family that we can contact? I am sure they would want to know what has happened to their daughter.'

'No, there isn't any family, unfortunately,' Ava replied, adding 'she is like a daughter to me, though.'

'Well, as there isn't any family, are you happy for me to discuss her injuries with you, Mrs Richards?'

'Yes, of course, Doctor, she will be moving in with me when she comes out of the hospital. I will be looking after her.'

'Going back to the morning, Mrs Richards, when you found Isobel; you had told the matron that she collapsed in your arms? He began to make notes.

'She was going in and out of consciousness, Doctor, she was very dizzy, and her body was shaking. Once we arrived here, I think she was awake; it was hard to tell with her swollen eyes. She hasn't spoken a word to me or anyone else since she has been here. I have just been sitting with her for an hour, and still nothing.'

'Isobel has been through a terrible ordeal, Mrs Richards, and when people have been through what she has, it will take time to respond to others. She could be reliving her ordeal over and over again. As far as physical injuries, there are several bruises to the upper part of both arms, which are consistent with being held down by force: you can still see the finger marks on the skin. One or more hard blows have caused injuries to her face. She has a nasal fracture and swelling on her eyes resulting from the blow. Once the swelling reduces, the bruising will come out and may look worse for a while. She also had a split lip which required two stitches.'

'Oh my goodness, Doctor, how long will it be before she can come home?'

'I don't think you fully understand the seriousness of Isobel's injuries, Mrs Richards.'

Ava looked confused.

'Yes, but she is young, and her face will heal in time, and the bruises will fade surely?'

'Mrs Richards, Isobel was viciously attacked in her room in the middle of the night.'

'Yes, I understand that Doctor; I don't quite understand what you are getting at?'

'There is no easy way to say this.' The doctor took a moment, to collect his thoughts. 'Isobel has been attacked in her bed. She was punched in the face, almost certainly twice, she then became unconscious and – whilst unconscious …

The doctor paused, then continued, '… she was raped, Mrs Richards. Her legs, especially her upper thighs, are red and bruised, and she has sustained severe internal bruising.'

'Sadly, this could affect her for a very long time; it might not, only time will tell.' Seeing Ava so upset, he tried to reassure her. 'I am so sorry, Mrs Richards. We have not spoken to Isobel yet: we thought it might be better coming from a family member or, in your case, a close friend.'

Ava looked at him with dismay and sadness. 'So what are you saying, Doctor? Will she recover?'

'Time will tell, I am afraid,' repeated the doctor, shaking his head.

'Thank you, Doctor, for being so candid. I *will* tell her, but perhaps not yet. Let's get her back to my home first. When do you think she will be well enough to leave the hospital?'

'Her superficial injuries should heal in two to three weeks, but her other injuries, well, who can tell? You can take her home in a couple of days, Mrs Richards; I will ask the matron to arrange the paperwork.'

'Thank you, Doctor, thank you for your help.'

'Alas, Mrs Richards, we are seeing too many of these cases in our hospital lately, a sign of the times Mrs Richards, a sign of the times.' The doctor shook his head slowly as he left the room.

Ava needed a few moments to compose herself whilst trying to process the shocking news. She was so angry at the monster responsible for ruining this poor girl's life.

When Ava went back to the ward to try and speak to Isobel, Matron drew the curtains back, and Isobel was now sitting up in bed. Taking Isobel's hand in her own, Ava explained that the hospital would allow her to come home in a couple of days.

Perhaps, she thought, *this might be a good time to ask if she would like to come back with me to Sunbird House?*

Waiting patiently for a response, she eventually heard a whispered reply, 'Yes, please.'

'That is great news, Isobel. We will take one day at a time, OK?'

Kissing her friend on the forehead, Ava asked if she wanted the rest of her possessions collected from the room.

'Yes, please, but not the bedcover.'

'Of course. We will soon have you in your room at Sunbird House; please treat it as your own.'

Ava could see the pain in Isobel's eyes, it was unbearable and she prayed for something to make it stop, but all she could do now was to reassure her as best she could.

'I will see you tomorrow; I hope you get some rest,' she said, as she left Isobel in the capable hands of the matron. Looking across as she left the ward, she could see Matron heading over Isobel's bed.

Reassured that Isobel was being cared for well, Ava returned to York Road to collect the remaining items. She wasn't relishing the idea of going back in the room, especially now, and once in there she quickly gathered the last articles and placed them in a box. Ava soon realised how little Isobel possessed: a picture of her grandmother, a jewellery box, and a few clothes. After one final glance around the room, she left, vowing never to step foot in that dreadful room ever again.

Once back at Sunbird House, she called for her housekeeper, 'Bo, Bo, are you there?' After a few moments, Bo appeared from the kitchen. 'Bo, we will be having a guest arrive tomorrow. She has not been well and will recuperate with us. So can you please make up the Honeysuckle Room; she will be comfortable there, overlooking the garden. Don't forget to use the best bed linen, the white embroidered bed cover. Also, can you please ask Cheng to cut a small posy of flowers tomorrow, perhaps a tiny bunch of the Chinese honeysuckle? It has such a sweet fragrance. But they must be fresh, so tell Cheng only to cut them in the morning. You will find a small cut crystal vase in my room; please use that one. Oh, and can you order a whole cod from Mr Myat, and some shrimp? Make sure it's from the morning catch, Bo, and check in the larder for fish paste. I think one of your lovely fish curries for her first meal would be most welcomed, Bo. We need to build up her strength.

'Yes, ma'am, I will see to that. What is the lady's name, ma'am?'

'Isobel, her name is Isobel. Just call her 'Miss Isobel'.'

'Yes, ma'am.' Bo then walked up the vast marble staircase to prepare Isobel's room.

Ava knew how lucky she was to have Bo and Cheng; they were not just the housekeeper and gardener, they were her friends. They had been with her for many years: Mr Philip, as they affectionately called him, had employed them soon after buying Sunbird House.

Cheng and Bo were husband and wife and had been allowed to live in the small gatehouse on the grounds. They had continued to work for Ava after Mr Phillips's death and had watched as she grieved for her beloved. Bo did worry about Ava: she had become a recluse in her own home, not seeing friends or family. It was so sad. Sunbird House had always been full of love and laughter, and they had especially enjoyed the summer dances in the ballroom; Mr Phillip had allowed them to have the evening off to enjoy the fun.

Flowers had draped the marble staircase: honeysuckle, roses and greenery intertwined the teak balustrades, all from Cheng's garden. Then, dressed in the finest couture of the day, Mrs Richards would descend effortlessly down the beautifully decorated staircase to the rapturous applause of her guests.

Bo remembered looking across at Mr Phillip on one such occasion and seeing his face; he adored his wife, they loved each other so very much.

It had been so sad when Mr Phillip died.

She remembered that, after his funeral, and once everyone had left the wake, she watched Mrs Richards walk alone around the house and could hear the window shutters being closed, one by one. She then heard Mrs Richard's bedroom door close, and that is where she stayed for one long month.

A close friend of Mr Richards had stepped in temporarily to look after the business until Ava felt strong enough, but when that would be, nobody knew.

Bo prepared meals and left them outside Mrs Richard's door, though she barely ate enough to keep a bird alive. She always made a point of going back to the big house every evening to check all was well, and on some evenings, she could hear Mrs Richard's sorrowful cries coming from the small connecting room to her bedroom. Originally it had been used as Mr Richards' dressing room, and it adjoined their master suite. But now Bo didn't know what she used it for, as she always kept it locked away from prying eyes. Finally, Bo was given strict orders not to allow anyone to go in there, which she obeyed, respecting her employer's wishes.

After several long weeks of mourning, Bo clearly remembered the day when Mrs Richards had re-opened the shutters, one by one. She had then announced that she would like breakfast on the back veranda, a special request which Bo had been delighted to hear.

Everyday life returned to Sunbird House, and Cheng once again brought cut flowers into the house, filling every empty vase. The floral aroma reached every corner of the house. A reluctant chapter of life without Phillip had begun, with Bo and Cheng right by Mrs Richards' side.

Once able, she took over the reins of the business again and immersed herself in work. She seemed happy enough, but Bo knew she would never be the same now that Mr Phillip was dead.

After a while, there was a slight change in her behaviour, and Mrs Richards introduced a gentleman to them. His name was Mr Peters. They married soon after; it was a small private ceremony with just two witnesses. Bo knew Mrs Richards didn't want a fuss.

Mr Peters was a very caring man, he looked after his wife and was very kind to Cheng and Bo. Unfortunately, he became ill, and Mrs Richards nursed him for over a year until he eventually passed away. When he died, it was a sad day, and Mrs Richards was alone again.

Bo thought Isobel being at Sunbird House would be great company for Mrs Richards, and was happy to help with the preparation.

Everything was ready and prepared now for Miss Isobel's visit: Bo had aired the room, the shutters were open, and the bed had been made up using the best linen. Cheng had his orders, too. The following morning, he was to cut fresh honeysuckle for the vase by the bedside table. Extra food had been ordered and delivered, including the fish that Mrs Richards had asked for, and placed in the cold store.

Bo and Cheng were ready and were now waiting to meet Miss Isobel; once again, there was great excitement at Sunbird House.

12

All Good Things Come to Those Who Wait

Williamʼs day was about to get better. He had always known that one day his big break would come, and today was that day.

It was Friday morning, and as he started his walk to work, he hadnʼt gone far when two of his co-workers rode past on their bicycles, shouting, ʻWell done, William!ʼ

Turning around to see who was behind him, he shrugged it off. Thinking he had nothing to be congratulated for and that he must have been mistaken for someone else, he continued his walk to work.

He clocked in as usual and was about to head down to the port side when he saw Mr Simmons approaching him. Everyone knew you only had a meeting with him if his dismissal was imminent, so William tried hard not to make eye contact.

Was he about to be dismissed? How could he tell Catherine? Especially now the baby was on the way? Williamʼs palms began to sweat as Mr Simmons reached out to shake his hand.

ʻWilliam, please follow me to my office.ʼ

William obliged and followed him into the corridor, passing several doors with polished brass nameplates. *They must be important employees to have their names on the door*, he thought to himself. *Perhaps one day my name might be on a highly polished brass plaque; perhaps not today though, if I get the sack!*

As he followed behind Mr Simmons, he looked to his left; the wall only came to waist height, allowing a large window to run the length of the building.

So this is where they have been watching me from, thought William, looking out at the view of the port side.

Mr Simmons turned right into his office, and William followed him in, taking the seat opposite the desk, noticing that he, too, had a highly polished brass plaque.

'Well, William, I am sure you are wondering why I have called you here?'

'Yes – have I done something wrong, Mr Simmons?'

'Now, what makes you think that, William? No, no … quite to the contrary. It's what you've done *right*, my boy,' he said, smiling.

'Sorry? I'm confused.'

'Well, you have worked for us here at The Indian Timber Company for – how long now?' Mr Simmons looked down at William's employee report. 'Let's see … ah, there it is, fourteen years, fifteen in September. You have been an exemplary employee, and as a reward for all your hard work, we have decided it was time you had a promotion.'

'Thank you, sir,' replied William, in disbelief at what he was hearing.

'Yes, William, you're a clever man, and we have been watching you. Shall we say you have a certain presence amongst the men? You always manage to get more out of them, much more than any of us can, and productivity is up. The time between receiving the rice, sorting, grading, bagging and loading onto the ships has improved to the point where we are ahead of our schedule. It's quite incredible, William: people seem to do whatever you ask of them.'

William was good at his job and was fully aware of how well he managed the other workers.

Mr Simmons continued, 'So, William, because of all of this, we would like to offer you a promotion to Wharf Manager. Your wage will be considerably higher. Now, how do you feel about that, William?'

For the first time in his life, William was speechless; had he heard correctly? So many thoughts were going through his mind that he couldn't find the words to reply. After a few moments, he composed himself.

'Well, I don't quite know what to say, Mr Simmons, thank you very much.'

'Oh, and also, before I forget, there is a house attached to this position. The street is very nice, all very similar houses and far superior to what you are used to, I daresay.'

'I don't know quite what to say,' William repeated.

'Well, as long as you say "yes", and accept the job, then I will start the paperwork.'

'Of course, yes, thank you so much,' William said, shaking Mr Simmons hand vigorously.

'Great, we will sort out the paperwork, and your new position will start on the first of next month. After that, we will give you a chance to pack up your current house and be ready to move into your new one.'

'Thank you again,' William said, as he left the office. Walking back down the stairs onto the wharf, he was still in a daze from the good news.

The sun was shining hard down on the river, and William knew it was going to be another hot and humid day. He could see several ships in the distance making their way down the river as he dodged the crowds of Indian port workers, pushing large carts piled high with white sacks of rice. Rolling his sleeves up, he was ready for another busy day in the blistering heat. Except that this day was different. All those years of back-breaking work had paid off and, at last, his big break had arrived. Once back on the port side with Mr Simmons' words still ringing in his ears, the dust and noise didn't seem to bother him, and the constant movement of trolleys and people back and forth around the wharf were not enough to distract him from his thoughts. Nothing was going to stop him now: he was going to be the new Wharf Manager!

The steam fuelled ships were chugging out great clouds of black smoke, and the thick smell of coal hung in the air. They were jostling for position, eager to unload and reload their cargo for destinations far away.

William had heard the workers joke about the last wharf manager. They had all laughed at him for wearing a suit and carrying a clipboard, and he could be spotted a mile off, sweating profusely.

They'd better not laugh at me, William thought, not relishing the idea of being the joke of the harbour. *I will soon sort them out; nobody will be laughing at me.*

The port workers graded the rice into various sacks at the other end of the wharf, ready to load onto the trolleys. William worked here; he had to pack them fast and ensure the correct order went to the right ship.

With a massive pile of rice in front of him, he and his co-workers – many of them Indians – laboured exceptionally hard to get the orders out. William was amazed at how his colleagues never asked for anything: not a pay rise, not better working conditions, nothing. The manager gave the lucky ones the job of looking after the elephants. They would train the animals to lift teak logs off the smaller boats and onto the waiting carts. The noise of the elephant trainers shouting their commands to the elephants, and the iron chains around their loads rattling all day long until dusk, had become part of his everyday experience.

Some of William's friends were amongst the hundreds of Indian workers brought across to help with Rangoon's expanding port. They were humble people, and he became angry when he heard rumours of their mistreatment. But, what could he do? He was not going to cause trouble: The India Timber Company were paying him to manage these people.

He occasionally looked up from his task in hand to see several ships coming closer down the Rangoon river, laden with cut teak logs that had been felled further up in the hills. Once unloaded, they would be processed on the port side, ready for export. So Rajan and his fellow elephants continued their steady work along the port, with their trainers directing them using large sticks.

William had worked so hard for the last fourteen years, and he wouldn't allow anything to spoil this moment of joy. He couldn't wait to tell Catherine his great news.

What a difference this will make to our lives! he thought. As he continued his work, his fellow workers patted him on the back and congratulated him on his promotion all day long. Finally, as the sun was setting and he watched the last ship of the day chugging its way down the river, he grabbed his jacket and went back up to the office to collect his new contract from Mr Simmons' secretary. Miss Roberts also gave him the address of his new house.

'Well done, William, well deserved,' she said.

'Thank you, Miss Roberts, my wife will be so pleased.' William left the office and headed home as fast as he could.

Catherine was collecting her washing from the line behind the houses when she heard William calling her name. Just as she put the basket down on the chair, William flew through the door, ran across the kitchen, grabbed her around the waist and waltzed her around the room.

'William!' she laughed, 'What are you doing? Put me down! Whatever has come over you?'

'Catherine, my darling Catherine, my beautiful wife carrying our child, you will never believe what happened today!' he shouted, at the top of his voice.

'What is it, William?'

'William, tell me!' desperate to hear his news.

'You had better sit down, Catherine,' he said, pulling a chair out for her. Kneeling in front of her, he said, 'Catherine, do you remember all the times I have said to you about having a house with a garden, with you sitting and drinking tea? Do you remember, Catherine?'

'Yes, William, I do remember, and I have always said that, as long as I have you, that is all I need.'

'All our dreams have come true! They promoted me to Wharf Manager! As a result, my wages will double, and I will never have to work nights again. Our money worries are over, Catherine: you won't need to wash or make clothes for other people anymore. We can live comfortably on my wage. What do you think, Catherine – isn't it great news?' William asked eagerly.

'William, that *is* fantastic news, well done,' she replied, trying to process his words.

'You *are* pleased, Catherine, aren't you?'

'Of course, William; it's a shock, that's all. It's a lot to take in,' Catherine replied. She saw her small sewing business ending, just like that, dismissing all her hard work.

See her reaction, William quickly responded, 'Of course, if you would like to continue the sewing business, you can; it might just be for a better clientele, that's all. You can't be making clothes for the street children anymore.'

Catherine had never allowed money to change who she was or how she treated people. Her family had money and she had a privileged childhood, but money had never

96

been Catherine's top priority. The love of a good man was enough for her, and she had William. They might have struggled financially, but as long as they had each other, all was well.

Was her life going to change so much because they now had money? Catherine was worried, she had seen how money changed people – and not always for the better.

Would it change them?

'I loved you before your promotion, and I love you now; you will always be my William. I am very pleased for you.'

'You should be pleased for both of us!'

'Yes, I *am* pleased, William, truly I am. It's just … I love our life exactly how it is, and perhaps with more money, it will change.'

'Well, while I was accepting this new promotion, Mr Simmons informed me that there is a house attached to the job!'

Catherine looked confused, 'So we have to move, William. Is that what you're saying?'

'Yes, Catherine, we have been given a beautiful house with a garden; I know you will love it!'

Without giving Catherine a chance to reply, he grabbed her hand, 'Don't say anything now: at least have a look first.'

Leading her outside, he slammed the door shut and flagged down a passing rickshaw, telling the driver the new address.

'It's not far: just by The Royal Lake. I know you will love it, Catherine!'

A few weeks later, The D'Souzas said their goodbyes to Halpin Road and moved into their new home. Catherine felt sad to leave: she loved their old home and had worked so hard building her small sewing business. Saying goodbye to her neighbours was difficult, too. She had grown close to them all, especially the children. As she put the last box on the truck and turned to say goodbye to her little house, three of the neighbours' children came and stood in front of her, each clutching an assortment of flowers in their tiny hands.

Promising herself there would be no tears, she thanked them for their gifts and kissed them all. As she climbed into the van, all her dear friends stood by their gates and waved her goodbye. Giving them a small wave in return, she looked away, unable to face them with tears in her eyes. She prayed the move to this fancy new house would be the making of her and William, but knew that her heart would always be in Halpin Road.

After a few weeks, and a little gentle persuasion from William, Catherine slowly settled into her new home and was beginning to enjoy her new surroundings. The rooms had been newly decorated, and with the extra money William had from his new wage, they were able to buy some new furniture.

The baby's room was painted in a pale lemon: the perfect colour for when the sun flooded the small nursery. By the afternoon, the sun moved to the back of the house, making the room more relaxed for naps. The cot was placed in the centre of the room and made up ready using the hand-sewn cot sheets and a small white blanket, embroidered with a lamb on the corner. Yards of white muslin draped the canopy and dropped to the floor.

Seeing there was still plenty to do, she continued to paint the wooden shutters white and, whilst she painted, she reflected on William's behaviour since moving here. To say he was a changed man was an understatement; he was so much happier and relaxed and, thankfully, there was no need for him to work the night shifts anymore, much to Catherine's relief. Every morning he left for work at six, arriving back home by six in the evening: perfectly timed to share an evening meal. This never happened at Halpin Road.

The day of his promotion, William had told her how he'd borrowed somebody's bicycle and rode home as quickly as he could to tell her the news. She laughed as she remembered, picturing him rushing into the house. He had been beside himself with excitement, grabbed her hand, and they had danced around the kitchen.

As they had arrived at the house, the first thing Catherine had noticed was the red roof, then, as they walked around the house, she saw the wraparound veranda. She had always dreamt of having one, and now it was hers. They had continued into the garden, full of beautiful plants, and she had been able to smell the honeysuckle in the air. Two teak trees stood tall on either side of the house, like two tall soldiers on guard.

It was love at first sight, and she remembered hugging William, telling him how much she loved it. William's dream had come true, she thought, laughing to herself: he always said it would, and it did!

Deciding to rest, Catherine put the paintbrush down and looked out of the bay window to see William in the front garden tending to the plants. It was Sunday, his only day to rest. *What a joyous sight that is*, she thought.

William was so happy with their new house, and he was either decorating or gardening every free moment. As he surveyed his garden, he could see several climbers had taken hold, with clusters of red flowers clinging to the pale yellow stone. 'Combretum Indicum,' he said, proudly.

He had been trying to learn the Latin names of the plants in the garden to impress Catherine, one of the trees was a highly prized teak. It was native to Burma and stood tall and straight beside the house with large green, fanned leaves reaching high above the roof.

William's new job was going well, except for the odd bit of ridicule from the workers, but he had been expecting some of that: after all, it wasn't so long ago that he was one of them. Wearing the suit and the starched collar had all been part of his big dream, but now, in reality, he thought he was going to melt under the blistering heat. It would take time for the men to accept him in his new position, he knew that.

Life was looking good, and he was to become a father a few weeks from now.

William knew Catherine would make an excellent mother, but would he be a good father? Only time would tell.

A few weeks later, Catherine awoke and felt unwell. She managed to get out of bed, made her way to the bathroom, and called for William. But, unfortunately, he had already left for work, leaving her in the house with Suhani, the housekeeper.

William had insisted Catherine had some help and did not want her in the house on her own all day. Catherine had accepted his decision and, as her pregnancy progressed, she decided having Suhani around had been a good idea.

'Suhani!' she shouted, holding tight onto the sink.

'Yes, ma'am, I am here!' the girl called, running up the stairs.

Suhani held Catherine under the elbow and led her back to the bedroom, only stopping briefly to see an emerging puddle of liquid appear by Catherine's feet.

'Don't worry, ma'am, that's your waters breaking, it's quite normal, don't worry. I've helped my mother deliver a few babies,' she reassured Catherine.

'Oh, Suhani, thank you, that is good to know. You must try and get hold of Mr D'Souza.'

'Let's get you back to bed; then I'll fetch the doctor. But, first, I'll make you some raspberry leaf tea. Then, I'll get a message to the doctor. The delivery boy should be bringing my fruit soon, I'm sure he'll go for a few rupees.'

'Thank you. I don't know what I would have done if you weren't here.'

'You're welcome, ma'am. Now back to bed and try and rest; I will be back shortly.'

Suhani ran back down the stairs, praying that the delivery boy would be on time for once. Luckily, as she entered the kitchen, she could see the errand boy, barefoot, running up the dusty path with an enormous sack balanced on his small shoulder.

'Faster boy, faster, I have an errand. I need you to run,' she shouted, 'and I will give you one rupee if you go as fast as you can.'

Although already struggling with his load, the boy attempted to speed up for the last few feet of the path. Then, carefully placing his goods by the door, the boy stood patiently for his orders. Suhani took a small purse from her apron pocket and placed the coin in the palm of his outstretched hand.

'Now listen carefully: go straight to Mr Williams, the doctor, and tell him Mrs D'Souza's baby is on the way. Do you understand, boy?' The boy nodded; she continued. 'Then, go to the port, look for the big office with red bricks and lots of windows – it has a metal staircase – go up to the top and tell one of the people in there that William D'Souza is needed at home urgently.' She looked at the boy – did he understand? She prayed that he did.

'Now, take the bike by the gate. If you do what I have asked, I will give you two rupees on your return.'

The boy's face lit up, and he shouted, 'Yes, ma'am!' as he ran down the path and jumped on the bike, peddling frantically out of the gate.

At least he understood the word rupee, but will the men receive their messages? she asked herself.

The doctor and Mr D'Souza should be here soon, she told herself.

Going back into the kitchen, she put the kettle on the stove, made up a tray with a small china teapot and cup, a jug of water and a glass, and took it up to see how the patient was coping.

'Oh, Suhani, did you get a message to William and the doctor?' Catherine asked anxiously, hoping for good news.

'All taken care of, ma'am, now don't you fret, it won't do the baby any good now, will it?' Suhani said, trying hard to remain calm herself.

'No, no, of course, you're right,' Catherine replied.

Suhani sat Catherine up gently and plumped the pillows behind her, then poured a cup of tea. So much to do, where would she start? Helping her mother was one thing, but delivering a baby on her own was another. What if the boy just took the money and ran? What if the doctor didn't get here on time? What if something happened to Mrs D'Souza or the baby – or both? Her mind was in turmoil. The panic was rising, until she thought, *what would my mother do? Think Suhani, think.*

Taking a few deep breaths, she went to the linen store and took out some old sheets for the bed, several towels, and a facecloth. Running back down to the kitchen, she grabbed a pile of old newspapers to cover the mattress. Once back in the bedroom, she asked, 'How are you feeling, ma'am?'

'I am getting some terrible pains in my back,' Catherine replied.

'I will get some Tiger Balm; I won't be long.'

Passing the nursery, Suhani quickly popped her head in the door. *How pretty the room looks*, she thought, looking at the white cot with the muslin canopy, but she didn't have time to dawdle; she quickly found the pot of balm and went back to Catherine's room.

'I will have to move you into the chair ma'am; you can look over the garden.' She gently helped Catherine out of bed and moved the chair to give a view of the garden, thinking perhaps it might take her mind off the pain for a bit of time.

Stripping the bed, Suhani laid several layers of newspaper over the mattress.

Suhani went downstairs again, hoping to see if anyone had arrived. Looking nervously at the clock above the range, she knew time was moving too fast and with no sign of help. She could hear Catherine calling her. Up to the bedroom she went again, saying 'I am going to fetch my mother. She is only down the street at Mrs Carter's house. Please don't move around whilst I am gone, I will be as quick as I can.' Before Catherine had time to think, Suhani had turned and run down the stairs, two at a time.

Catherine watched her run down the path and out through the gate, suddenly realising she was alone in the house and praying to God that nothing would happen until Suhani got back.

Suhani ran as fast as she could and within a few minutes was knocking frantically on Mrs Carter's door. She heard a man's voice shouting as he approached the door whilst she caught her breath.

'Whatever is wrong, is there a fire? I'm coming, I'm coming!'

As the door swung open, Suhani could see a tall older gentleman with a large moustache and an angry face glaring at her.

'What is it, girl? You come knocking on my door; you know you should use the servant's door at the back! Anyone would think you were one of us!' he yelled.

'Sorry, Mr Carter, but I need my mother,' Suhani said, stepping back from the door.

'You need your mother, girl? Well, *I* need her to finish her chores for which I am paying her!' Mr Carter replied angrily.

'Who's at the door, darling?' called a voice from within the house.

'Blasted servant girl from up the road, you know – the young couple who moved in a while back.'

'Well, what does she want, Peter?' the woman asked, sounding slightly irritated.

'She wants her mother. Damn cheek, if you ask me,' he snarled. 'Be away with you, girl, wasting my time,' he shouted and began to close the door.

Suhani called, 'But I need her, Mr Carter, it's urgent.'

Mrs Carter suddenly appeared at the door, shooing Mr Carter away and saying, 'Oh, for goodness sake, Peter, go back to your paper! I will deal with the girl. Now, what is this all about?' she asked, looking down at Suhani.

'Thank you, Memsaab, my mother is needed over at Mrs D'Souza's house; the baby is coming.'

'What on earth could a civilised woman like Mrs D'Souza possibly want with your mother? She doesn't need witchcraft, or whatever you people do. She needs a doctor; we *do* live in a civilised society here, girl!'

'Yes, Mrs Carter, we have called for the doctor and Mr William, but they have not arrived, so I need my mother to help me with Mrs D'Souza.'

Suhani was pleading now, acutely aware of time. Seeing the urgency in the girls face, Mrs Carter begrudgingly said, 'Well, all right, your mother may help since it's urgent for Mrs D'Souza: we don't want people thinking we are not good neighbours. But, your mother's working day has only just begun; I will have to deduct the time from her wages. You may meet her at the servant's door.' And with those harsh words still fresh in the air, she slammed the door in Suhani's face.

She had become accustomed to the British treating her Indian community poorly, always looking down their noses at them as if they were second class citizens. They all worked hard for the British: her father and brothers worked down at the port alongside many other Indian citizens. Not wanting to be left in India alone, Daya had decided to accompany her daughter to work in Rangoon.

Suhani hadn't seen her father or brothers in months; she knew the port owners worked them hard and had heard the scary stories circulating in the community of overcrowding and inadequate treatment.

Finding work had not been too difficult for her. Being young and healthy had helped her prospects, and when Mr and Mrs D'Souza were looking for a young housekeeper to help with the baby when it arrived, it seemed the perfect job for her. She had heard about the job from the fishmonger that delivered to the D'Souza house. The Carters treated her mother like a common slave, so Suhani was expecting similar treatment, but much to her surprise, the D'Souzas were very courteous and kind – especially Mr D'Souza, who was very handsome.

Rushing round to the servants' door, she met her mother coming out and explained what had happened at the D'Souzas house. She spoke in Urdu to her mother as Daya didn't speak English, much to the disgust of the Carters.

They walked as quickly as they could and, upon approaching the house, saw Mrs D'Souza at the bedroom window. She tried to wave but held onto the window ledge in pain. Once in the house, they rushed into the kitchen. Daya filled a basin of warm water from the kettle on the range and asked her daughter for some rags, adding one of Mr William's leather belts to the list. Suhani looked at her strangely but did as she was told. She called out for Catherine as she began climbing the stairs.

'Ma'am, I have brought my mother to help,' Suhani said as they entered the bedroom.

'Thank God you're back,' cried Catherine; she was now leaning over the bed in pain. 'Where is William? I need him here?' she cried.

That morning, William had gone to work blissfully unaware of how his day would unfurl. An early morning meeting with one of the ships' captains had kept him out of the office and on a steamer. William had been in his position of wharf manager for six months now and was beginning to relax a little and enjoy his newfound power.

He told Catherine it was all about negotiating, moving workers, keeping the ship captains happy, and keeping his manager Lucas happy, though William had instantly disliked the man. He was arrogant and British, which he assumed gave him the upper hand. However, William knew he had to prove himself to Lucas, and did a pretty good job. Lucas's job was the next step for William on his journey to the top. Lucas might have thought *he* was William's master, but time was, too. He had to be quick and think on his feet: looking across at the port, hundreds of steamers were all jostling for position, hungry for their cargo. But he loved every minute of it, and this new power he was given was very satisfying. In the fourteen years William had been at the port, he had always been at the manager's beck and call and had been the whipping boy. But now, if anything went wrong, it was his turn to shout the orders, and it felt good.

After finishing his meeting with the captain, he made his way back to the office. It was midday, and he was more than ready for a cup of tea.

'William!' a voice shouted from behind him. He turned and saw Miss Roberts running towards him, looking very hot and flustered.

'Oh, William, we have been looking for you everywhere!'

'I'm sorry, I was on board The Thistle with Captain Mortimer; we were negotiating prices to carry the rice to Madras. Is there a problem?'

Miss Roberts stopped, caught her breath and looked at William. 'You need to get home, William. I think your wife is having a baby. We tried to find you earlier, but nobody knew where you were.'

The blood drained from William's face. 'Do you know what time the message arrived?' he asked, trying to remain calm.

'I think it was about an hour ago, William, try not to worry. First babies always take their time; go now, and give Mrs D'Souza all our best wishes,' Miss Roberts replied, sitting down on the nearest chair.

William grabbed his jacket and left the building in a panic, running down the stairs and out onto the wharf, the crowds of workers pushing past him, carts laden with rice sacks getting in his way. 'Move out of the bloody way!' he shouted, desperate to get to Catherine.

Spotting an old bike propped up by a pile of wood, he grabbed it and pedalled home as fast as he could, passing the bike's owner on the way out.

'Oi, that's my bike! Thief! Somebody stop him!'

William shouted back, 'Emergency, you'll get it back tomorrow!' The bike owner threw his cap to the floor in anger, but William was already halfway home.

Meanwhile, Catherine's contractions were becoming closer together. Suhani's mother, Daya, squeezed a facecloth out in the bowl of water and dabbed Catherine's forehead as she spoke to her in a quiet, calming voice in Urdu. Although Catherine only recognised a few words, it seemed to calm her down.

Meanwhile, Suhani kept looking for the men or the boy, but still nobody. *Whatever has happened to that little scrap? He won't be getting his money!* she thought.

Catherine called out in pain and Daya told her daughter to help Mrs D'Souza onto the bed: it was time.

Catherine began to cry. 'The doctor's not coming, is he? Where is my husband?'

The contractions were closer now, and Suhani looked to her mother for reassurance. Daya took the leather belt off the table and handed it to Catherine, telling Suhani to explain that it was for the pain.

'My mother has delivered many babies; you are in safe hands. Now, when my mother nods, bite down on the belt and push down, but not before,' she said, holding Catherine's hand.

Her mother positioned herself at the end of the bed and, after checking to see how dilated Catherine was, spoke to Suhani, who then translated her words. 'When mother nods, you start to push.' Catherine was frightened but had no choice but to follow their instructions.

Mother and daughter moved to either side of the bed, asking Catherine to bring her legs up and push her weight onto them. All three of them waited in silence for the next contraction, and as it began, Daya nodded for Catherine to push – and she did, with all that she had. As labour moved on and the pain became more intense, Catherine put the leather between her teeth and bit down hard with the next contraction.

They don't know what they are doing, William; where are you?

They heard the sound of tyres on the gravel outside; Suhani rested Catherine's foot back onto the bed and ran over to the window. As she leaned out, she caught a glimpse of Mr D'Souza as he ran into the house. Not wanting him to see Catherine in the throes of labour, she ran down the stairs and met him halfway.

'Where is my wife?' he demanded, desperately trying to see over her shoulder.

'Ma'am is nearly ready to meet your baby, Mr D'Souza; please stay down there, go in the kitchen, and I will call you as soon as I can.'

'But I need to see her, is she all right?' he implored.

'Mrs D'Souza is doing just fine, now go to the kitchen, and I will fetch you when the baby has arrived.'

Suhani walked down the stairs into the kitchen with William and settled him down at the table with a cup of tea and the newspaper. Her mother called her name from upstairs and their eyes met; she could see real fear in his eyes.

'He must love her,' she thought.

Leaving him in the kitchen, she turned and said, 'Try not to worry; Mrs D'Souza is in good hands. When the doctor arrives, can you please send him up?'

William looked at her in shock. 'What do you mean "when the doctor arrives"? Who is helping Catherine? Oh my God, she needs a doctor! Suhani!' Jumping off his chair, he ran up the stairs and made it to the landing before she could stop him.

'Please, Mr D'Souza, your wife is very close. My mother is with her now.'

'Your mother! Oh my, oh my!' William placed his hands on his head and paced up and down the landing.

'She has delivered many babies, Mr D'Souza, please don't worry,' Suhani replied, trying to reassure him.

Her mother called for her to help and she implored William to wait where he was. Hearing all the commotion, Catherine then cried out, 'Please, William, do as she says, please!'

Not wanting to distress his beautiful wife anymore, he held his hands over his ears to block out her cries and ran into the nursery.

What happens if I lose my Catherine? Or our baby? Or both? he thought. Falling to his knees, he began to pray for forgiveness.

'Forgive me, father, for I have sinned. I have betrayed my wife; I have lied and cheated all our married life. If you can hear me, forgive me of my sins. I promise I will never stray again. I do not deserve her or our child but I cannot lose them; I implore you, I beg you to forgive my sins. I will repent. Take me, not my wife, not my child.'

William bowed his head. He was so ashamed of his past: the lies, the drinking, the gambling, and numerous affairs – too many to count. Tears streamed down his face as he remained on his knees, repenting his sins. He would give it all up in a heartbeat if it meant they were safe. From the depth of his penance, a pure sound emerged: it was the sound of a newborn's cry. Lifting his head, he wiped the tears from his face, scrambled to his feet, and ran to the landing just as Suhani left the bedroom.

'Congratulations, Mr D'Souza, you have a beautiful baby girl.'

William raised his eyes to the heavens and thanked God for hearing his prayers.

'William, William, is that you? Come in,' an exhausted voice called.

As he walked into the bedroom, he saw Catherine sitting up in bed with a small bundle in her arms. Suhani and Daya finished cleaning Catherine up and then took everything back down to the kitchen. At last, they were alone, just the three of them: Catherine, William, and their beautiful baby girl.

'Oh, William,' she cried, 'Oh, my William, I was so frightened.'

'You're safe now, Catherine, my darling Catherine.' His eyes filled with tears again as he leaned over and kissed her gently. Then, looking down at the tiny bundle in her arms, he kissed his daughter. 'You are amazing, Catherine, my beautiful wife.'

'We have a beautiful baby girl, William. Can you believe it?' Hold her, and say hello to your daughter.'

Lifting her from Catherine's arms, he carried his sleeping newborn to the cot in her nursery and laid her down gently so as not to wake her. Stepping back, he gazed at this tiny newborn child, perfect in every way. He was the happiest man in the world.

Carefully unwrapping her from the shawl, he marvelled at her tiny body. He checked her ten fingers and ten toes and touched her perfect little head and her cute button nose. A mop of curly black hair crowned her face, and as she slept, he noticed her long dark eyelashes resting on the top of her cheeks. He watched her slight chest rise and fall with each breath, her mouth suckling on an imaginary breast.

How could such a beautiful little miracle belong to me? he asked himself, *such perfection and so tiny. I don't deserve you.*

Gently wrapping the baby back in her shawl, he pulled the canopy back over the cot and quietly left the room. Seeing that Catherine had fallen asleep, he kissed her and whispered, 'Thank you.'

He needed to see Suhani and hear about the morning's events, but as he reached the bottom of the staircase he saw a suited man approach the front door. William soon realised it must be the doctor, who looked very flustered. *By the look of him, the gossip could be accurate*, thought William, *I am sure someone called him a bumbling idiot, too full of his importance.* He chuckled to himself as he opened the door.

Most of Catherine's appointments had been at the hospital during her pregnancy, so this was the first time William had met the local doctor. The man stood in his doorway dressed in a heavy dark suit, looking extremely hot and bothered as he dabbed the sweat from his forehead with a handkerchief.

'Good afternoon, Doctor,' said William, extending his hand. The overweight and the overheated man took William's hand and replied.

'Good afternoon, Mr D'Souza, my name is Dr Williams. There seems to have been some confusion this morning; I thought you were someone else, my fault entirely. There used to be a Mr D'Souza down Halpin Road, and his wife was called Catherine; a poor little couple. I think he was a port worker, and she took in washing; they wouldn't have been able to pay my fee, that's for sure. Damn port workers keep having children they can't afford. So I thought I ought to go there anyway, customer relations and all that, and I got all the way there in a rickshaw, only to find they had moved! Damned waste of my time. Oh, I am sorry, there's me rattling on, please forgive me …

'What a beautiful house you have here, sir, yes, beautiful!' he continued, admiring the large, bright hallway. 'You called for me to come and see your wife: I believe she is in labour?'

William stood on the doorstep; he could feel the anger rising in his gut. *No*, he said to himself, *that is not the way to behave, not now you are a man of means*, so he held his tongue.

'My wife sent a message to you at eleven o'clock this morning, Doctor; it is now three in the afternoon. Luckily for you, we had some expert help, and the baby has been delivered. Mother and baby are doing fine.'

Feeling somewhat uncomfortable from hearing this news, the doctor replied, 'Please accept my sincere apologies, Mr D'Souza; there has been a dreadful failure in communications. Would you like me to check everything is fine with your wife, completely free of charge, of course?'

'Thank you, Doctor, that would be greatly appreciated.' William called for Suhani. 'Please take the doctor upstairs to see Mrs D'Souza.'

She nodded, and the doctor followed her up the stairs.

What a day! thought William, as he walked back into the kitchen. Suhani's mother, Daya, a petite Indian lady dressed in a dark green sari, stopped cleaning up and turned to William.

Walking across the kitchen, he extended his hand for her to shake; he didn't know what else to do. Daya wiped her hands dry on her apron, took his hand and raised it to her forehead, smiling.

'Thank you, so very much,' William said, not knowing if she understood him or not. They looked at each other and words were not necessary.

Daya beckoned him to sit down, which he did, exhausted from the day's events. Lunch had already been prepared for Mrs D'Souza to eat and, not wanting to waste it, Daya filled a large bowl with the steaming fish curry and placed it in front of William.

He soon succumbed to the delicious meal and the aroma of chilli, coriander and salmon filled the kitchen. Just as he finished the last morsel, Suhani informed him that the doctor was now leaving.

Wiping his mouth on the napkin, William pushed the chair back and went into the hall.

'Well, Mr D'Souza, I am delighted to say mother and baby are well; you must have had professional help. Can I ask which hospital's doctors helped? I hope you don't mind me inquiring?'

William signalled Suhani to fetch her mother from the kitchen and, holding her hand, brought Daya out to see the doctor. He watched the doctor's face intently as he came to the realisation that this petite Indian woman delivered babies just as well as any hospital doctor. *What a picture*, thought William, laughing to himself.

'I see,' said the doctor, looking somewhat embarrassed by the whole situation. 'Well, goodness me, girl, please congratulate your mother. But perhaps in the future, it might be best to leave these matters to the professionals.' He then made his way to the door.

'Thank you for your help, even though it was a little late,' said William, as the doctor shuffled out of the door. 'Oh, and by the way, Doctor,' William continued, as the doctor turned to look at him, 'just a tiny point to correct you on: the couple in Halpin Road, you remember – the port worker and the washerwoman – I know where they have moved to.'

'Oh, really, Mr D'Souza, and where would that be?' inquired the doctor.

'Here, Doctor! Catherine and William D'Souza live here!' and with those satisfying words still on his tongue, William promptly slammed the door and went upstairs to see his wife and child.

Lucas, William's boss at the port, tried his hardest to torment him, but William ignored him and simply continued to work hard. He had met his type before, all hot air and no substance. He thought Lucas too self-assured and arrogant for his liking, and hadn't worked his hands to the bone for some little upstart to get in his way for future promotions.

Fellow workers agreed with William; they all hoped Lucas would get his comeuppance one day. Being the son of the new chief of police allowed him the freedom to lord it over others. It did not make him popular, however, and William in particular did not like him at all.

Thankfully, times were changing fast in Rangoon, and for William it opened up opportunities that he could never have imagined. Not even Lucas was going to get in his way. *He needs to watch his back*, thought William, after yet another day of bullying.

William did have in his favour that he worked so hard, rolling his sleeves up with the other workmen when needed, and by doing this, he had gained much respect from all. However, no matter how hard he worked in his new position, it never seemed good enough for Lucas.

'William, why haven't you finished the schedule for tomorrow's moorings?' Lucas shouted to William over his workers. Having already had to hold his tongue many a time for, fear of telling Lucas what he thought of him, William replied, 'Yes, sir. I will get it finished now.'

'You need to smarten yourself up, Mr D'Souza! Your timekeeping is getting slack, Mr D'Souza! We don't pay you to stand idle!'

Lucas was trying his damnedest to wear him down, but William knew he was more intelligent than this and had to bide his time.

Home life was difficult, too. He didn't understand why; after all, his new position was paying a good wage, they lived in a beautiful house, Catherine was well looked after and wanted for nothing. Their beautiful daughter, who they had called Agnes, brought them such joy every day. He didn't understand why Catherine was unhappy. She was distant towards him: perhaps *he* was the problem?

Seated in the dining room, the D'Souzas ate their evening meal in silence one warm summer evening. There seemed to have been a lost connection between them and William was shocked, as he had always thought Catherine would love him forever.

He sensed the atmosphere was not conducive to an entertaining evening ahead, so he decided to take in the air after his meal.

'I might go and have a stroll around the park, just to get some fresh evening air, if that's all right with you, Catherine?' he asked.

'Yes, that's fine. I was going to have an early night; I have a lot of orders to get through tomorrow,' she quickly replied.

Catherine seemed almost pleased he was going out and somewhat relieved that she didn't have to spend more time with him. However, he had noticed a look in her eyes, flat and unemotional.

'You do know I am very proud of you, Catherine, don't you? You have built your business up from nothing – and now look at you, making suits for the government's officials.'

'Thank you, William,' she said, then she kissed him on the cheek.

It had been a long time since any physical contact had happened between them, and William was surprised, though it was only a passionless peck on the cheek.

Perhaps I should not go out tonight? he thought, *but she doesn't want me here, does she?* He pondered for a few moments and said, 'I won't be long. Will you still be up when I get back?'

'I have some orders to finish off; then I will have an early night, William.'

He had his answer, not the one he was hoping for, so he walked through the hallway and quietly closed the front door behind him so as not to wake Agnes.

As William took a slow walk towards the Royal Lake he was surprised at how quiet it was, especially for a town that never slept. The moon's reflection rested on the black water, illuminating his walk to the water's edge. Sitting down, he lit a cigarette and took a long slow draw, exhaling into the darkness.

His beloved pagoda across the water, a vision in the distance, still shimmering in the moonlight, was still his favourite place to relax and gave him time to think.

As he exhaled, a long stream of smoke snaked its way through the air in front of him, and through the smoke, he could make out a figure walking towards him.

Flicking the cigarette into the water, he stood up and took off his jacket.

'I didn't think you were coming? What a pleasant surprise,' he said as he laid his jacket on the grass.

'Thank you, William,' she replied, taking his hand.

'I hope it wasn't a problem getting out?'

'Why would it be? It's my night off after all.'

Their shoulders touched, his body yearning for physical contact; he turned and kissed her, desperate for her to reciprocate.

'We have to be careful, William, people might see us.'

'Don't worry,' he said, 'I have a plan so we can spend more time together, away from prying eyes.'

'Oh, William, that would be wonderful. Do you remember our first kiss?'

'Of course, my beautiful girl.' They kissed before she spoke again.

'It was in the garden, I was hanging out the sheets and you kissed the nape of my neck.'

'I remember,' he recalled, as his hand slowly moved from her neck to her breasts.

'Yes, William,' she panted, 'can you believe it? We have been together one month today: it's our anniversary.' He kissed her again.

Suddenly, the pair heard voices in the darkness and, quickly composing themselves, turned their faces away from the emerging couple. Once they had gone, William kissed her neck and slowly moved his hand up her thigh but she grabbed it, saying, 'Not here, William.'

He stopped immediately and reached for his jacket, and without uttering a word, turned to go.

'I am sorry, William, but anyone could see us, please understand.'

Without acknowledging her response, he changed the subject.

'I'll be free tomorrow lunchtime for an hour. Can you get to York Road?'

'Well, I suppose so; I could run some errands. Why?'

'You'll find out if you turn up. You *do* want to spend more time with me, don't you? So meet me at the bottom of York Road at one o'clock.'

Knowing she would be there, he smiled confidently, kissed her on the cheek and walked back home.

Once back at the house, he had a momentary pang of guilt. But Catherine had been so distant and hadn't shown him any affection for so long now. What was a man to do? He had tried to kiss her on several occasions, but she had turned away, seeing almost repulsed by him. He didn't want to betray her or go behind her back, but he had needs, and she couldn't or *wouldn't* meet them. She had left him no choice.

The following day, true to his word, William met the girl at one o'clock at York Road. He walked in front so as not to draw attention. Following a few feet behind, she walked to the end of the road, turned into the courtyard, and followed him up the metal steps to a room at the top.

It felt strange for him to return to the room, as he recalled the last time: eager to see Isobel, only to be greeted by an empty room and a door unlocked. He had left in a rage, imagining Isobel was getting up to all sorts of lurid behaviour with other men. Slamming the door behind him, he had rushed back down onto the street and had the misfortune of colliding with Ava. He had washed his hands of Isobel now: she meant nothing to him and could rot in hell as far as he was concerned. Now he had another beautiful girl in that room, which made him laugh. He liked her feistiness; William always loved a challenge. Holding her hand, he led her to the bed.

At last: some privacy, he thought.

Once on the bed, he attempted to seduce her but to no avail; she pushed him off and laughed, 'I am not that sort of girl, William.'

'Are you teasing me?' he asked. Perhaps it was too soon, but it wasn't long before he worked his magic on her, and she was ready for him. As they lay on the bed in an embrace, she could feel his heartbeat and wished they could stay like that forever. But William broke the silence by looking at his watch and started to get up, 'We have to go, Suhani. We can't stay here all day: people will get suspicious.'

'Can we come back here again, William?'

'Of course we can. This will be our little love nest.' He leant over and kissed her gently. 'I will go out first, wait five minutes, and I will see you tonight back at the house.'

On his way back to work, William began to think about how strange it had been back in the room; it had felt as though Isobel's presence was still there. He didn't have time for such thoughts, however, and he dismissed them as sentimental nonsense.

Suhani was thrilled to be William's secret lover and would happily become the new Mrs D'Souza when the opportunity arose, making her days as a servant girl numbered. Like William, she too had big dreams. He made her feel special, and she had fallen in love with him. But for now, she had to bide her time, as William had told her; *Our relationship is much more exciting when it's a secret.*

As he left, she could hear the sound of his footsteps disappearing down the metal stairs. Still having errands to run, and worried Mrs D'Souza would be wondering

where she had got to, she quickly dressed and left the
room.

13

A Special Guest

Ava went upstairs and inspected Isobel's room; she needed to check that everything was in order. Bo had made the bed up using the best white linen as ma'am had asked her, and Cheng had gathered some fresh honeysuckle and left it on the kitchen table, ready to be arranged.

Perfect, thought Ava, as she looked around the room.

Leaving the house for the hospital, she gave the driver his instructions. Once there, she signed the relevant paperwork for Isobel's discharge in Matron's office and went to the ward to collect her. As she approached the bed, she could see that the nurse had pulled the curtain around Isobel. Quietly calling her name, Ava pulled the curtains slightly open and stepped through the gap. Seeing Isobel sitting on the edge of the bed, she looked so small and childlike with her back to Ava; she was dressed in a light blue frock, and her small case on the floor beside her brought a lump to Ava's throat. It was the only dress she had managed to get from the room, not wanting to spend a minute longer than she had to in that dreadful place.

Ava moved around the bed to see her. 'Isobel, are you ready to go?' She could see that Isobel was deep in thought, staring out of the window.

'Yes,' she replied, picking up her small suitcase; taking Ava's arm for support, she left the ward.

The journey to Sunbird House passed in silence. Isobel said nothing, deep in thought, looking out to nowhere. Once they arrived, Ava helped her down from the rickshaw.

'Welcome to my home, Isobel, please treat it as your own.'

'Thank you, Ava. Is it OK if I could go to my room now?'

'Of course, I will take you there now. It's a lovely room, Isobel, it overlooks the garden at the back and will be quiet for you.'

'Thank you,' Isobel replied, her head bowed for fear of eye contact.

Ava led her up the grand staircase and they continued along the marble landing until they reached Isobel's room. Stopping at the door, she looked up and noticed a miniature oval painting of honeysuckle painted in green and vibrant yellows, and there was a small plaque with 'Honeysuckle Suite' painted in gold paint below.

'Here we are,' Ava said, opening the door, 'you have your bathroom to the left.' She indicated another door, which was half open. 'My housekeeper Bo will bring you some tea shortly, and if you feel up to it, please come downstairs. We could have tea on the veranda: what do you think?'

'Can I please have it in my room?' Isobel quietly replied.

'Of course, whatever you want, please make yourself comfortable, and if you need anything, just ring the bell by your bed. I will go and arrange some tea for you now.' Ava left the room, closing the door quietly behind her.

Bo had heard them enter the house and, having anticipated the need for a strong cup of tea, was standing by the stove. The kettle had just boiled, and she poured hot water into two small teapots: one for Ava and one for her new guest, Miss Isobel.

Ava let out a long sigh, sitting at the scrubbed kitchen table.

'Thank you, Bo. I was hoping she might have wanted to have tea with me when she first arrived. Perhaps I am expecting too much from the poor girl. Oh, Bo, all the wonderful sparkle has gone from her eyes.'

'Don't worry, ma'am, she is a young girl; give her time. She will soon be sitting having tea with you, just need time.'

'Of course you're right, Bo, as usual: we will have to be patient and give her time.' Pouring herself a cup of tea, Ava watched Bo make up a small tray for their new guest, which she then took up to her room.

Knocking on the door, Bo heard a quiet voice reply, 'Yes?'

'Morning, Miss Isobel, I have brought you some tea and a small piece of sanwin makin; it's ma'am's favourite, I thought you might like it too.' Entering the room, she placed the tray on the small table and introduced herself, 'My name is Bo, I am the housekeeper.' She then pointed towards the opened window, 'When you look out the window, you may see my husband Cheng; he is the gardener. Please ring the bell if you need anything, Miss Isobel.'

'Thank you,' came the reply.

Bo smiled and left the room.

Sitting back in the chair, Isobel viewed the lush green garden and, just like Bo had said, there next to the flower border, tending to his plants, was Bo's husband, Cheng. He was so immersed in his plants he hadn't noticed Isobel watching him. A warm breeze drifted over her, and as she sipped her tea, she slowly began to relax. Ava had been so kind, letting her stay in her beautiful home, she thought.

After a few minutes, however, the darkness came again and thoughts of that awful night flooded her mind in full colour, as she shut her eyes as tight as she could, trying to block out the vision in front of her. But it was to no avail, she was in the darkness, fighting for her life. Her breathing became laboured, and she moved away from the window onto the bed. She climbed under the covers and curled up as small as she could make herself, so small that she thought she would disappear and nobody would notice. But, instead, she cried deep, mournful sobs, grieving for her previous life before all of this hell. The crying continued until she was completely exhausted, and she fell into a deep sleep.

Bo collected the uneaten food tray left at Isobel's door the following morning. She heard crying, so she decided not to disturb. Ava wanted to ensure Isobel was all right before leaving for work, so she took the breakfast tray from Bo and went up to the Honeysuckle Suite. She knocked quietly but heard no reply. Still worried, she opened the door and was surprised to see Isobel sitting in the chair by the window.

'Good morning Isobel, I have brought you some breakfast. Is it all right if I come in?'

'Yes, please come in, Ava.'

'I have to go to work now, Isobel, but Bo and Cheng are here if you need anything, and if you feel up to it, Bo can arrange lunch or a cup of tea in the garden; it's a glorious day.'

'I am OK, thank you, can I stay in my room?'

'Yes, of course, there is no rush. If you like reading, please take a look in the library. I will see you tonight.'

It might do me good to stretch my legs; it feels like I have been in this room forever, Isobel thought.

Once Ava had left for work, Isobel heard distant voices from the garden and waited for silence. Then, barefooted, she stepped out onto the cold marble floor and tiptoed along the landing to the far bedroom. Entering the room, she saw the bright morning sun streaming through the opened shutters, catching the crystals on the chandeliers and creating hundreds of tiny sparkles that bounced off the white-painted ceiling. It was a beautiful room. Moving to the velvet chaise longue at the end of the bed, she sat down and admired the

129

ornately carved teak four-poster bed with its beautifully embroidered throw in turquoise silk. In the corner of the room was a black and red chinoiserie cabinet inlaid with mother-of-pearl.

How beautiful, thought Isobel, *this has to be Ava's bedroom; she has such exquisite taste.*

A dressing table sat between the two large windows, and as Isobel tentatively sat down on the stool, she picked up a small silver box next to the mirror. Curiosity got the better of her, and she opened it. Seeing several pearl and jade earrings, Isobel lifted one to her ear. She was shocked to see a pale, drawn young woman with fading bruises looking back at her from the mirror. Quickly putting the earring back, she noticed a small brass key at the bottom of the box. Placing it in the palm of her hand, she began to wonder which door it belonged to.

Hearing voices coming from the entrance hall, she placed the jewellery box back on the dressing table and tiptoed back to her room, closing the door very quietly behind her.

Her heart pounded through her chest. *What was I thinking? I should never have gone into Ava's room.* Looking down at her hand, she soon realised she still had the key! *Ava told me to explore her home, so I wasn't doing anything wrong. I just need to get this key back into her jewellery box*, she thought, trying to convince herself.

But then, there was a knock on her door. 'Come in,' she said, sitting up on her bed, quickly slipping the key under the pillow.

'I have your lunch here, Miss Isobel.' Bo entered and placed the tray on the table. 'You come to the garden, Miss Isobel?'

'Maybe tomorrow, Bo.' She wasn't ready to step outside quite yet.

'Ok, maybe tomorrow.' Bo then returned to the kitchen.

Whilst eating lunch, Isobel began to think. Why was a key hidden at the bottom of the jewellery box? Which door would it open?

After lunch, she quietly tiptoed back along the marble-floored landing and slipped the key back under the earrings in the jewellery box.

Later that evening, Ava returned from work and went straight to see Isobel. She had hoped she would be feeling a little more relaxed and would have begun to eat. But, feeling guilty, Isobel decided to tell Ava she had been in her bedroom and looked through her jewellery box.

'I said you can explore, that's fine.'

'Your bedroom is lovely.'

'It is my favourite room. Please don't worry: I said you should treat this house as if it were your own. I am glad you feel comfortable leaving your room. There is *one* room, however, I have locked for personal reasons. I hope you will respect my privacy and not go in there.'

'Of course,' Isobel replied.

Is this the room with the secret key? But which room is it? thought Isobel before, as if she had read her mind, Ava replied.

'It's the small dressing room attached to my bedroom. Some things have to remain private; you do understand, don't you, Isobel?'

'Yes, of course, that's fine Ava, we all need our privacy at times.'

After they said their goodnights, Isobel laid on her bed, and a blue haze from the moonlit sky lit her room. The opened window allowed a warm breeze to flow over her, and she drifted into a peaceful slumber.

Isobel desperately fought for air, shrouded in darkness and pinned to the bed. A menacing black shadow hung above her as she screamed to be released, but she made no sound. All she could hear was laughter, a man's laughter; it was getting louder, and louder, and louder.

Finally, with a gasp of air, Isobel sat bolt upright, her body covered in sweat, breathless with tears streaming down her face. It was another nightmare with the same awful vision of darkness and helplessness. Pulling the covers over her head, she began to feel a little calmer, repeating to herself: *this is a safe place, this is a safe place, this is a safe place.*

After several minutes of trying to calm herself down, her thoughts were disturbed by the faint sound of crying coming from somewhere nearby. She put on her dressing gown and tiptoed out onto the cold marble landing. The house was silent except for a distant sound coming from Ava's room. Walking slowly down the corridor, the marble cold on her bare feet, she hesitantly entered Ava's bedroom and saw a chink of light under the secret room's door.

Ava must be in there, she thought, listening intently to the crying for a bit longer. It felt wrong to be eavesdropping on someone else's pain, so she swiftly tiptoed back to her room and gently closed the door.

Poor Ava, thought Isobel, *she always looks so happy.* So what could be the reason for her to be so upset? And what was so private in that room that it needed to be under lock and key?

14

Fallen Ashes

Sunbird House had begun to feel like home for Isobel. It had taken her a while, but with Ava's kindness and love, she was starting to feel like her old self once more.

Putting that dreadful ordeal to the back of her mind, she was determined to move on and, if she continued to do well, would soon be able to return to work. The love and respect she had for Ava grew, and she was in awe of the older woman's tenacity and determination, working long hours and taking on ever-increasing workloads.

Ava was a very determined woman, and she had become one of the most successful women in the fabric world.

Isobel wanted to try and repay all the kindness that Ava had shown her whilst living at Sunbird House. It was a beautiful Saturday morning, and she had decided to help Bo in the kitchen. Once there, she was happy to be busy again as she gathered all the items for breakfast.

'Is it OK for me to help?' she asked, looking at Bo, who by now was smiling at her.

'Of course, Miss Isobel, we can make the table upon the veranda. Ma'am will be so pleased for you to join her.'

They busily prepared the tray, and Bo added a small vase filled with yellow roses picked by Cheng from his rose garden. Isobel laid the crisp white linen tablecloth over the wicker table, and Bo lay the table. Ava stepped onto the veranda from her morning walk around the garden, just as they had finished.

'Good morning, everyone,' she said, pleasantly surprised to see Isobel out of her room. Bo went to fetch the tea and the small pot of mohinga.

The sun was still rising, and the warm air was pleasant with its sweet aromas wafting from Cheng's rose garden. Sitting down, they admired the beautiful garden that wrapped itself around the house. Ava turned to Isobel; it was lovely to be together for breakfast.

'You look so well! How are you feeling?'

'I am well, thank you for asking, and thank you for everything you have done for me. I don't know what would have happened to me if it wasn't for you.'

'I couldn't leave you in that dreadful state.' Ava quickly changed the subject. 'We must now think about the future, she said, raising her china teacup. 'To the future, my darling girl.'

'Yes, to the future.' Isobel raised her teacup to meet Ava's.

Her life was turning around, she felt happy again and now wanted to repay Ava. But the thought of Ava breaking her heart, night after night, was almost too much to bear. There *must* be a way to stop her from being so sad, and Isobel was determined to find it.

When the house was empty, and Ava had left for work, Isobel checked downstairs. Bo had left for the market, and Cheng's bicycle, which he propped up against the garden wall near the back door, was gone. She could now appreciate the house in all its glory and silence. The sun shone through the glass atrium above the entrance, sending shards of light to illuminate the marble floor below.

Bo had told her stories of the beautiful parties held at Sunbird House. She pictured Ava in a beautiful flowing dress, slowly descending the sweeping staircase to her adoring friends and her beloved husband. Bo had also told her how poor Mr Phillips had died, and of the intense love he and Ava had for one another.

Isobel wondered if she would fall in love with anyone again. Her heart had been broken and stamped on by the one person she thought had loved her. How wrong could she have been? Dismissing her thoughts of him, she continued with her plan as she knew she was against the clock. She retrieved the key from the jewellery box and went straight to the dressing room door.

Was she doing the right thing? She wasn't sure. But she needed to find the reason for Ava's crying. Nervously, she tried to put the key in the door, her hands still shaking, and tried again. It fitted perfectly. Taking a deep breath, and with great trepidation, Isobel turned the key, and the door opened.

She was greeted by the sight of a dressmaker's dummy dressed in the most exquisite white lace and chiffon wedding dress; she had never before seen anything so beautiful. Moving closer, she noticed a long lace and voile veil attached to the dummy's back. It fell in soft folds down to the floor, and the hem of the wedding dress spread out like a pool of water.

Sunlight shone through the gaps in the closed shutters and caught the hundreds of hand-sewn crystals on the veil. The pearl and crystal-encrusted bodice must have looked stunning on Ava, and Isobel pictured her on her wedding day as a beautiful bride. Looking to her left, she saw a male dummy dressed in an entire morning suit: trousers, a fitted waistcoat and a morning jacket, all in immaculate condition. Placed on the floor in front of the dummy was a pair of highly polished shoes, and a dried rose was still attached to the jacket's lapel; Isobel wondered if it had come from Cheng's garden.

This must be Ava's and Phillip's wedding attire, Isobel thought, *how sad it looks now; it's a constant reminder of what she has lost.*

An ornately carved teak desk was by the window; its top drawer was open, and a pile of letters peeked out. Taking a note off the stack, Isobel read: *To my darling husband, Phillip.*

Next to the desk was a black lacquered table, and on that table was a white glazed urn. Gold leaf decorated the lid, and a miniature painting of a golden bird decorated the front. An inscription below read: *Fly free, my love, till we meet again.*

An overwhelming sadness washed over Isobel, and her eyes began to fill with tears. *Poor Ava, she loved him so very much, but this is too sad.*

137

Leaning over the desk to put the letter back in the drawer, she suddenly heard Ava's voice.

'What the hell are you doing in here?'

Isobel was so startled that she swung around immediately, still with the letter in her hand, and as she turned, she caught the side of the urn. Both women watched in horror as the pot fell to the floor, smashing into pieces. Ava saw its contents, her beloved Phillip's ashes, spilt out onto the hard wooden floor and scattered over her delicate wedding dress. There were no words to describe the moment, only silence followed by a heart-wrenching cry.

'Get out, get out!' Ava screamed, tears streaming down her face. 'Look what you've done!'

'I am so, so sorry, Ava, it was an accident; I didn't mean ...'

Ava cut Isobel's words dead. 'Get out, get out!' she cried again, as she ran to the wedding dress and the broken urn. Slumped on the floor, she tried in vain to retrieve the ashes.

Isobel ran out of the room and down the stairs. Bo had heard the commotion upstairs and was already by the kitchen door.

'I am so sorry, Bo, please tell Ava it was an accident, I didn't mean to break the urn.'

Bo rushed up to the room with Isobel following behind, and as they reached the dressing room, she turned and said, 'Better you go to the room, I see to ma'am.'

'Of course,' replied Isobel as she walked back to her room, stopping momentarily at the doorway and watching as Bo knelt beside Ava and put her arms around the sobbing woman.

'Oh, Bo!' she cried, 'I have nothing left of him now; I have nothing.' She buried her head in Bo's shoulder. Her loyal housekeeper rocked her like a mother rocks a baby, speaking softly to comfort her.

Isobel couldn't watch any more and went into her room, closing the door quietly. Running to her bed, she buried her head in the pillows: nobody needed to hear her crying.

Isobel didn't sleep much that night, reliving the accident with the urn repeatedly in her head; she could see Ava's face with the tears flowing down her cheeks and a look of absolute despair. Ava had been so upset, and knowing it was all her fault just made it worse. If only she hadn't let curiosity get the better of her. She deserved to have been shouted at, and had decided that it would be better for everyone if she left.

Pulling her case out from the cupboard, she began to pack, though she had no idea as to where she would go. She needed to leave; at least, then, she couldn't upset anyone else.

There was a knock on her door. Bo walked in with a tray and, seeing the suitcase, said, 'No need for this, you speak to ma'am, it is ok.'

'I don't think so, Bo, Mrs Richards was so upset; I don't think I can make it better. What was I thinking? I wanted to help her, she has been so kind to me, and I heard her crying in that room. I thought perhaps I could in some way help her. I have made such a mess of everything.'

Isobel sat on the bed and began to cry. Bo turned to see Ava standing in the doorway; she had been there long enough to have heard their conversation.

'I am sorry I shouted at you, Isobel, it was just the shock of seeing Phillip's ashes on the floor and over my dress. Please don't go.'

'I don't know how to make this better, Ava. I can't. I just wanted to help you, and then it all went wrong. It's better if I just go.'

'But where will you go? Please stay here with us; we can put all of this behind us. I have had all night to calm down and … I need to thank you, Isobel.'

Shocked by her response, Isobel replied, 'How can you possibly thank me, Ava, after what I did? Accident or not, I should not have gone into your room, especially after you specifically asked me not to.'

'I have had time to think. Phillip loved life and lived it to the full – we laughed and danced and drank wine: perhaps a little too much. But we lived, Isobel, *really lived*, and since he's been gone, my life has been working and home. There is no laughter, no dancing and no wine. I haven't lived. I merely exist; even my darling second husband couldn't bring me back to who I am. But last night, the shock of seeing Phillip's ashes made me realise: I, too, will become ashes. I have been mourning my past for so long now. I am tired. I have realised that no amount of crying will ever bring my Phillip back, so I need to live my life to the fullest while I can. I have *you* to thank for that.'

'I don't know what to say.'

'Well, you can stop packing for a start, and I think we should go on the veranda and have breakfast together. What do you think?'

Wiping her tears away, Isobel went over to Ava. They respected each other's pain, and each could feel that this was the beginning of a new chapter for both of them.

After a couple of weeks, Ava asked Isobel if she felt ready to go back to work. She decided she was ready and agreed to start back on the following Monday. She felt slightly apprehensive about going back to the shop, but Ava reassured her that she would be safe with her. Ava had even joked, saying that perhaps she should cut down on Bo's Indian sweets;kulkuls. Isobel laughed but had to agree: she had put on a little extra weight, but she reassured herself that the extra pounds would drop off once back at work.

Monday morning arrived, and they travelled together to the shop. Ava had an appointment to see a new manufacturer that morning. 'I shouldn't be gone too long; I will ask Lily to pop in to help.'

'I should be fine, Ava, honestly.'

'Well, there is still an awful lot to do, so she said she can pop in for an hour; I should be back by then.'

Lily arrived at the shop, and as lunch approached, Isobel decided to take her break. She was ravenous; she didn't know why. Bo had prepared breakfast for her that morning and she had tucked into it so surely she shouldn't be hungry again yet? Stepping out onto the street, she took a deep breath and strolled around the market. There was a familiarity within the busy market's hustle and bustle; the aromas and recognisable faces all reminded Isobel of 'him'. He had turned her whole life upside down – the man she had loved with all her heart had ruined her and treated her like a common whore.

15

Never Look Back

Isobel's life was so different now: she felt happy, and nothing could spoil it.

Finding herself in the familiar courtyard, memories came rushing back. Hearing footsteps on the stairs, she moved forward, and as she got closer, a man's voice whispered, 'Are you awake?'

She knew it was all in her imagination, but her heart still yearned for his touch. She had loved him with every inch of her body; he was her lover, friend, and confidant.

Pushing the door open, she stepped inside. Nothing had changed, the furniture was in the same place, even the candle was still in its holder by the window. She had lost count of the number of times it had been lit and placed there, praying for him to come and hold her. But the reminiscing had eventually stopped, and her love for him had fallen away like leaves from a tree.

Seeing the bedcover again ignited a dark memory that she would rather forget. Her breathing suddenly became laboured, as if a hand was pushing down on her mouth. Panicking, she reached for the door but then stopped; footsteps were approaching the room and were getting closer and closer. Where could she go? She looked desperately around the room. Where could she hide? She was trapped. *I need to get out!* she screamed, inside her head.

The owners of the voices were now outside the door. *Think, think! I do not want them to see me here!* Running to the bed, Isobel slid under it, just in time as the door opened. She held her breath. Thankfully the room was pretty dark, so she lifted the sheet slightly, only to see two pairs of shoes, one female, one male, just inches from her face. She froze.

'So this is what you had in mind! It's not quite a palace, is it?' the girl said, laughing.

'We could soon make it a little love nest!'

'That's all you think about, isn't it?'

'But I can't help it: you're so beautiful. I want you.'

They stopped talking and sat down and the bedsprings pushed firmly down onto Isobel's back; she wanted to shout. Then the man slipped off his shoes and they fell to the floor with a clunk; suddenly, it all felt very familiar. His voice, his laugh … and now, his shoes.

Oh my God, oh my God! Her head was spinning. *William, it's William!* she shouted silently, desperate to escape.

Eventually, the springs lifted off her back, and feet appeared in front of her once more.

'William, you know I'm not that sort of girl!' the girl laughed as she stood up from the bed.

'I know you're not; I just got a bit carried away, that's all. Now come here,' he said as he pulled the girl closer. Isobel couldn't bear to listen. Sitting back on the bed,

William picked up his shoe, his hand inches away from her face. She held her breath.

'I need to get back to work now. Can we do this again soon?' William asked.

'We will have to see, Mr D'Souza!' Her voice was almost childlike.

Isobel waited for the door to shut, and for the sound of footsteps to disappear. Clambering out from under the bed made her feel extremely nauseous and, without warning, she vomited all over the tattered rug.

William is doing it again! I can't believe he is with another young girl: how could he? He loved me! 'We can use this as our love nest ...'

Isobel hated him, but she hated herself even more forever having loved him.

She reached for the bed to sit down. The room started to spin, and she felt a warm wet sensation running down her leg and onto the floor. She realised the bed covers were wet too. Sweat ran off her face, and she closed her eyes in pain. What was happening to her? 'Help me, please! Help me!' she cried.

As she lay on the bed, the pain increased with every minute. Her life flashed before her, and she didn't like what she saw: a young girl full of promise meets a man who leaves her with nothing. She fought back; she did not want to die. Her cries became more desperate as time went on, but nobody could hear her pain. She was all alone.

Meanwhile, Ava had returned to her shop with several rolls of new fabric. 'Lily, can you help me? There are a few more rolls outside to bring in,' Ava asked, handing her some money. 'Can you pay the driver, please?'

Taking the new rolls of fabric to the stockroom, they stood them up against the far wall.

'Well, Lily, I have had a very productive morning. How has it been here? Have you been busy?' she asked, looking around the shop.

'We *have* been quite busy, yes.'

'Good, yes, that's good.' Looking around the shop, Ava noticed Lily was alone.

'Lily, where is Isobel?' she asked, somewhat concerned.

'Oh, she went to get some lunch in the market and hasn't returned since; I couldn't leave the shop as I was on my own.'

The colour drained from Ava's face. 'I will be back in a minute,' she said, and she rushed out of the shop.

She ran into the courtyard and up the staircase, and found the door closed. 'Good, at least she hasn't gone in there!' she thought, looking at the closed door. Turning to go back down, she heard a cry coming from the room. Turning the handle, she pushed the door open and saw Isobel writhing with pain on the bed. Rushing over, Ava was shocked to see her in this dreadful condition.

'What is it, Isobel? What's the matter?' Ava saw her clutching her stomach in agony.

'Help me,' she screamed, 'it's my stomach, Ava, help me!'

The memory of Phillip dying in front of her came flooding back; he had grabbed his chest just like Isobel was holding her stomach. She had been helpless to help

Phillip, as she watched his lifeless body, but now she *could* do something: she needed to help Isobel.

'It's going to be ok. I am here now,' she said reassuringly.

Quickly assessing the situation, Ava soon came to the shocking realisation that Isobel was about to give birth. Trying to remain calm, she said, 'now, let's try and slow down your breathing; it will help with the pain.'

Seeing the wet patch on the floor, together with Isobel's pains coming regularly, Ava knew she needed urgent help, but she couldn't leave her. As she tried to decide what to do for the best, she heard footsteps on the stairs and saw Lily standing in the doorway.

'Oh, Mrs Richards, I could hear someone screaming; I thought someone was attacking you! Are you all right?'

'It's not me, Lily, it's Isobel. Run, Lily, fetch the doctor as quickly as you can.'

Lily turned and ran down the stairs and into the market to fetch Dr Williams.

'What's happening to me, Ava? I'm frightened!'

Take a deep breath; I think you are having a baby,'

'I can't be Ava. I haven't, I mean the last time...' she stopped dead, staring at Ava in disbelief. Ava held her hand, 'I didn't know how to tell you, Isobel; I wanted to wait till you were stronger, I never in a million years thought you had fallen pregnant from it,'

'I knew,' she cried, 'I knew he had raped me,' and with those words barely off her tongue, she let out a piercing scream.

Ava looked down on the bed; she had given birth to a tiny baby; it didn't cry, it didn't move. Reaching for it

147

quickly, she picked it up and turned it over tummy down onto the palm of her hand, rubbing its back rigorously, using the bed cover. Isobel was still screaming whilst pushing out the afterbirth.

She then stopped; shock had taken over as she watched in horror, and Ava turned the baby on to its back; still not breathing, she could see its small lifeless body. Leaning over, she pressed her mouth over the baby's nose and mouth and gave a small but firm breath and then continued to rub its back,

'Cry, please cry!'

Reaching her hair, she grabbed the metal hair clip and managed to clamp the cord.

Time had stood still for Isobel as she looked on helplessly. Ava continued to rub the baby's back,

'Please God, please God,' she prayed, and after a few moments, its little lungs filled with air, and they both heard the baby's first cry.

Wrapping it up in her jacket, Ava looked at Isobel and announced,

You have a beautiful baby girl,' she said, her eyes wide open. Unable to move, the pain was still immense, and tears streamed down her cheeks. Ava prayed the doctor wouldn't be long, and soon she heard muttering from outside and recognised the voice as Dr Williams.

'Goodness me, what have we here?' he said, moving towards the bed with his bag.

'Good afternoon, doctor. We have a mother and her baby.'

'Ahh, Mrs Richards, goodness me. I haven't seen you for a very long time, yes, a very long time. If I remember rightly, it was an unfortunate time. Your husband, Mr Richards, had passed away so suddenly, yes, yes I remember now.' Ava cut him off before he continued with his babbling; they didn't have time to waste.

'We will need to get her to the hospital urgently,' Ava told him.

'Yes, of course, I will go and arrange that. I will just check that mother and baby are fine first if that is all right? Good use of a hairclip, Mrs Richards,' he said, laughing as he opened his bag and cut and clamped the cord. 'She is a little scrap, isn't she?'

Ava looked at him sternly and seeing her reaction, continued by saying, 'of course, all babies look like little scraps at first.'

'We need to get her to the hospital now; she is still in a lot of pain, Doctor. I don't know if we will be able to move her though, even the breeze on her skin is causing her pain.'

'How long was she in labour, Mrs Richards?'

'I suppose it can't be any more than a couple of hours.'

There's your problem: when a mother has her child so quickly, her body hasn't had time to catch up. I will go and make the arrangements' he said, adding, 'Goodness me, young lady, your husband will have a shock, hey?'

Isobel didn't reply, but Ava stepped in quickly, saying, 'I think she is still in shock, Doctor; we need to give her a little more time to get used to the idea.'

'Of course, of course, right! I will go and arrange the transport to get them both to the hospital,' he muttered, as he gathered his equipment and closed his bag.

'Thank you, Doctor,' Ava replied, relieved to see the back of him.

Once the doctor had left, the room returned to silence. Ava found a towel, wrapped the baby in it, and then handed her to Isobel, but she turned away. Ava thought she must still be traumatised by all of this, so she held the baby close and waited for the doctor to return.

It has been such a traumatic experience for this young girl; she just needs some time, Ava thought, as she looked down at the tiny innocent baby in her arms. *You didn't ask to be born, did you, my little one?* she mused, holding the baby girl close. Once at the hospital Isobel was sent to the maternity ward, with the baby being placed in the nursery.

Ava spent as much time at the hospital as she could work permitting, but Isobel had remained silent from the moment she had given birth. For Ava, this was all a new experience. She had never fed a baby or changed its nappy, and soon she felt a natural bond developing between them.

Ava decided to go to the hospital one morning before opening the shop. Carrying a basket full of fruit for Isobel and a small parcel wrapped in pink tissue paper for the baby, she approached the sister on the ward. After a few words and a small contribution to the nurses' fund, Ava was allowed to see Isobel for just a few moments.

Moving the curtain, she stepped inside and was surprised to see Isobel sitting up. Ava put her basket down on the cabinet beside the bed. 'I have brought you some lovely fruit Isobel, fresh from the market this morning.' Arranging the fruit in the empty bowl, she again tried to engage in conversation, but Isobel remained silent. Taking the small package out of the basket, she unwrapped the tissue paper and said, 'Look, Isobel, look at this exquisite little dress I bought yesterday from that little shop just down from me on the corner. Isn't it the prettiest thing you have ever seen?' She held up the tiny pink satin dress but Isobel didn't comment and simply continued to look out of the window.

Ava was in despair; what else could she do to make Isobel love her baby? Not wanting to nurse her or even hold her was beyond Ava's comprehension. They sat in silence for a while. Ava was concerned for the baby: if Isobel refused even to see her, what was she to do? Isobel eventually broke the silence.

'I think in the circumstances, it would be better for all concerned if a family could adopt the baby,' she said.

Ava had been expecting Isobel to say this, but she still prayed for a change of heart, especially if she held the baby. Ava tried to change the subject, not acknowledging Isobel's words. 'The doctor informed me you can come home tomorrow, won't that be lovely, Isobel?'

Ava knew that Isobel was struggling to do the right thing for herself and the baby. 'I think it's for the best, Ava,' she repeated, 'for her to be adopted. She would be a constant reminder of what happened, I know it's not her fault, but every time I look at her, I see him. You do understand, don't you, Ava?'

'Of course I understand, and it's your decision to make, but perhaps you could give it a little more time? You might change your mind.'

'No. I have made my mind up.' Isobel was adamant.

As they talked, she heard a commotion on the ward and pulled the curtain to one side. A nurse ran past them, heading for the nursery. Ava stood up to see what was happening and heard one of them say, 'it's Isobel's.'

As Ava ran towards the nursery, she saw one of the nurses picking up a baby and rubbing its back vigorously.

'Isobel!' shouted Ava. Isobel looked up. 'Quickly, it's your baby,' Ava repeated, 'She is your daughter! She needs you!'

Struggling to get off the bed, Isobel walked as fast as she could to get to the nursery. Ava grabbed her hand, and they stood there helpless, watching Isobel's baby fight for her life.

'Please don't let her die!' Isobel cried as she watched in horror.

The nurse continued to rub the baby's back. Isobel, distraught by now, held Ava's hand tight as the room fell silent. Everyone held their breath, willing the child to take a breath and after a few agonising moments the baby let out a shrill cry.

'She is a little fighter!' cried the nurse, 'I thought we lost her.'

Isobel shook as the nurse sat her down and handed her the baby. The tiny girl's eyes were open and looking straight at her. Lifting her, she kissed her tiny nose and whispered, 'Please forgive me.' Kissing her again, she carried her baby back to the ward.

'How could I give her up? She is my future; she belongs with me,' Isobel cried, trying hard to hold back the tears. 'She is my daughter. '

'Yes, she belongs to you, and whatever happens, that will never change, Isobel. She will have an amazing and happy life with such an incredible mother who will be with her every step of the way. Perhaps we need to give her a name: she is nearly a week old after all. Though I expect with all that's happened over the past few days, naming her might have been the last thing on your mind?'

'I *have* thought of a name,' Isobel said.

'How wonderful, and what are you going to call her?'

'I am going to call her "Hope", and every time I look at her beautiful face, it will remind me that from the deepest and darkest moments in my life, hope shines through. She will be my inspiration when life gets tough.'

16

The Sunbird

There was great excitement at Sunbird House for Isobel and Hope's return from hospital.

Bo, Cheng and Ava had been busy preparing for the new baby's arrival. They had set up a small wicker crib in Isobel's room, and Ava had been shopping for sheets, glass feeding bottles and cloth nappies.

Whilst shopping, she spotted the perfect gift for baby Hope: a beautiful bird made from felt and fabric, perched on a display box in the window. It had green velvet wings and a yellow satin belly. 'Goodness, it even has a blue throat, just like the real thing,' she cried.

Thrilled with her purchase, she asked to have it gift wrapped and couldn't wait to show Isobel.

Once home, she went straight to the kitchen, where Bo was preparing catfish for the evening meal.

'Bo, look what I found, isn't he exquisite?' she said, as she began to unwrap the tissue paper carefully. Bo wiped her hands on her apron, looking on with amusement. It had been so long since she had seen ma'am so excited. Ava removed the last piece of wrapping and held the bird up triumphantly.

'Look, I have managed to find Hope her very own sunbird!'

Surprised at the purchase, Bo retorted, 'Ma'am, he certainly is a nice bird, but Hope she chews him, baby eat everything!'

Disappointed at Bo's reaction, Ava sat down and held the bird in her hand. 'Oh yes, I forgot babies put everything in their mouths; oh well, he will have to go on a high shelf and watch over her,' she said, smiling.

Two days later, Matron discharged Isobel from the hospital.

The journey back to Sunbird House wasn't a long one, and as they turned into the drive, she looked at Ava and said, 'I don't know how I will ever be able to repay you, Ava. You saved my daughter's life, and you saved mine. I will be in your debt forever. My life would have taken a very different path, and not a good one, if we had never met. I shudder to think where I would have ended up.'

Ava was touched by her kind words; she looked upon Isobel as if she was her own daughter.

'You are both safe now, and that's the main thing.' Taking hold of Isobel's hand, she helped her down from the rickshaw. 'Shall we go home?'

'Yes, please, Ava,' Isobel replied.

With baby Hope in her mother's arms, they began the slow walk down the gravel path towards Sunbird House, to start their next chapter.

Isobel's love for Ava was extraordinary; she had been the only one that had cared for her and had come to her rescue when she so desperately needed help. She was grateful to her and wanted to be completely honest, especially now. Remembering back to the very first day she met Ava at her shop, she had been so nervous and very nearly talked herself out of going for the interview. When asked about her family, she had stupidly replied that she had none and was an orphan. The words had just flowed from her mouth, and she couldn't take them back. Now was the time to tell the truth, and ask Ava for forgiveness. Once settled back into their beautiful home, Isobel needed to pick her moment.

Ava asked Bo to set the table for afternoon tea on the veranda whilst they took a short walk around the garden. The air was warm, and the sun was glowing in the clear blue sky. Admiring Cheng's rose garden, they could see the clusters of old roses that clung to the stone wall by the back of the house. Their sweet perfume wafted in the air as they passed through the rows of ornate bushes laden with full blooms. Bo waved, and they made their way back under the shade of the veranda, sitting down on the comfy wicker seats with their large silk cushions.

Handing Hope over to Ava, Isobel nervously wrung her hands, knowing she had to start a difficult conversation. She began, 'I need to talk to you about something, Ava, and you might get angry. But before I start, I need you to know that I had my reasons.'

'This all sounds very serious,' said Ava, bouncing Hope on her knee.

'I don't know how to tell you ...' Isobel hesitated.

'I always find it's better to say what you have to say and then deal later with the aftermath.'

'OK ... well, do you remember the day I came into your shop for the first time? I was inquiring about the job you had advertised. Well, when you asked me if I lived at home, I replied that I was an orphan.'

'Yes, I remember.' Ava looked perplexed.

'I am so sorry, Ava; I feel dreadful. I have parents, and they live in Mandalay. I haven't seen them in such a long time. Once they knew about it …' Isobel stopped herself, realising she couldn't continue. She didn't want anyone to know about William.

Ava put Hope in the crib next to them; she gurgled for a moment then closed her eyes. Looking up from the crib, Ava casually said, 'I know, Isobel. I do my homework on all my employees.'

Isobel was shocked and concerned about what else she knew. Ava continued as she poured herself a cup of tea from the ornate teapot. 'I located your parents through a friend of mine, and I know how they disowned you once they knew you were with an older man. I will not ask you for the name of this man, that is your secret to keep. All I know is that you survived and are safe with me. If you would like me to, I can talk to your parents, perhaps see if they are willing to reconcile, especially now they have a granddaughter.'

Isobel sat back in her chair, confused but relieved at the same time. 'So all this time, you knew what was going on above your shop, and yet you never said a word.'

'It wasn't my place, Isobel; it is your life. I am only your employer, not your keeper.'

'You are much more than that, Ava, you have been like a mother to me, and I am so grateful for what you have done for Hope and myself.'

'Would you like me to contact your parents?'

'I don't think they would want to see me, Ava; I must be such a disappointment to them.'

'Leave it with me,' Ava replied, and leaning over the crib, she looked at Hope, who by now was fast asleep.

'I have to discuss something else with you Isobel and I have been trying to find the right time, but there is never a good time to say what I have to say.'

Isobel looked concerned and placed her cup on the table.

'What is it, Ava?'

'What did you know about the man you had the relationship with Isobel? You told me he cared for his grandmother?'

'Yes, he lived with her and looked after her. William was a very private man. I didn't really know him at all.'

'Isobel, I am afraid he had been lying to you about many things'

'What do you mean?'

'His full name is William D'Souza and he does not live with his grandmother, far from it: he lives with his wife, Catherine, who is a very close family friend.'

Isobel stared at Ava. 'But we talked about marriage and children. I thought we had a future together but then …' She looked away, too ashamed to say any more.

'Isobel, none of this is your fault. You were, and still are, a young woman who was taken advantage of, and I think you know that it was him that attacked you that evening and he is Hope's father.' Taking Isobel's hand, Ava said, 'Catherine is his wife and has been for many years, and they have a child.'

She could see Isobel trying to be brave and hold back her tears as she replied. 'Yes it was him, it was William, he raped me. I never want to see him again,' she cried, the tears flowing down her face.

Ava remained calm. 'Now that I know who attacked you, I will have to tell the authorities, Isobel.'

'Ava, please, you can't,' Isobel pleaded, 'everyone will know what he did to me, and then there's Hope to consider. Please, Ava, I am begging you for Hope's sake, do not go to the authorities.' Isobel was beside herself, frantically pacing across the veranda. 'The shame of it all, Ava, haven't I been through enough? It's more than I can bear!' she cried.

'I have to protect two people here, Isobel, you and Catherine. If you do not want anyone to know what happened to you or who is the father of your child, then you – or should I say we – will have to keep it secret. It will be difficult to keep the two of you from ever meeting and when Catherine visits Sunbird House you must ensure you are not here. She may well come to the shop but I will know that in advance. You could visit your parents, I am sure they would love to see their granddaughter. But you must promise me, Isobel, that you will never disclose the identity of your attacker or Hope's father. Can you do that for me, Isobel?' she asked, determined that Isobel understood what was being asked of her. 'If it ever came to light that you had broken our promise then I am afraid my loyalties would remain with Catherine and we will no longer have a friendship, am I making myself clear?' Ava felt wretched having to say this to Isobel, especially as she had grown very fond of her and Hope.

'I quite understand, Ava, I will not break our promise; your friendship means more to me,' she replied quietly.

'But what happens when Hope asks you questions about her father, or anyone else asks about him – what will you tell them, Isobel?'

Looking directly at Ava, Isobel replied coldly. 'I will tell them he is dead.'

They sat in silence for a while, each preoccupied with their thoughts, until Hope cried and the silence was broken. Isobel reached down into the crib and carefully lifted the baby into her arms. 'I will go to my room if that is all right, Ava?'

'Yes please do. It's been an exhausting morning.' Ava paused. 'You have done the right thing, Isobel, by telling me, your secret is safe.'

Leaning over, Isobel kissed Ava on the cheek. 'I don't know what would have happened to me if you hadn't come to my rescue, thank you.'

Ava watched them go into the house then poured herself another tea. The pot was cold but it didn't matter, there were more important things to worry about.

Ava sipped her tea and began to think about the task ahead. Firstly she needed to contact Isobel's parents and she knew that would not be easy, she would have to use her negotiating skills – but they hadn't failed her yet. Secondly, she needed to keep Catherine safe and the only way to do that was to keep a close eye on her. William had always made it difficult for their relationship, but between the two of them they had maintained a close and loving relationship with or without his consent. But now, everything had changed, including William's attitude towards her: she felt his distrust which only fuelled her determination to see Catherine more. He was suspicious of her, especially now, after she had caught him almost red handed. For once she had the upper hand and he would have to accept her now, or deal with the consequences.

Several weeks had passed, and Ava had, at last, had a conversation with Isobel's parents. They set a date to see Isobel and their new granddaughter, with one compromise.

After a few weeks, the day finally arrived, and Isobel nervously paced her room. She tried on numerous dresses, eventually deciding on the plain peach dress with the small embroidered flowers on the cuffs. She was desperate to make a good impression on her mother; perhaps she would see that Isobel had now grown up and become a responsible adult.

They were arriving at lunchtime, so Ava had asked Bo to prepare a beautiful meal for them all to enjoy. 'Good food is always a great ice breaker,' she had said. Cheng picked fresh flowers from the garden for the centre display, and Ava added the final touches, displaying her best china and crystal glasses, all gleaming in the morning sun.

Hope was bathed and dressed in her sweetest outfit, with a bonnet. She looked as pretty as a picture, sitting on a blanket under the shade of the tree.

Bo and Isobel were busy preparing a veritable feast for the guests, and there was a buzz of excitement and anticipation at Sunbird House.

Knowing how important today was for Isobel, Ava prayed it would succeed for all their sakes. By twelve thirty, all the preparations were complete. Ava had made a large jug of Pimm's for them all to enjoy and had added cucumber as a final touch.

Sitting under the large umbrella shade, they sipped the cool refreshing drink, rewarding all their hard work. Isobel lifted Hope off the blanket, ready to give her lunch, and as she turned, she saw her mother and father walking down the drive. Ava took the baby from her arms, and she went to greet them.

She had dreamed of this moment a hundred times in her head, and now they were walking towards her. Isobel's mother ran to her; they hugged and cried in each other's arms.

'I am so sorry for leaving as I did, Mother, I should never ...'

Her mother stopped her. 'It's in the past now, Isobel; we need to look to the future.'

Looking across at her father, Isobel wondered if he would be as generous as her mother. He had aged and looked uncomfortable. He had never been a man of many words but had always been a loving father. Taking his hand, she kissed it and looked into his eyes for forgiveness.

Putting his arms around her, he held her close and remained there for several minutes while Ava looked on and smiled. Finally, Isobel wiped her tears away and introduced Ava, Bo and Cheng to her parents.

'Well, I think we are missing someone very special,' her father said, 'where is my beautiful granddaughter?'

Isobel lifted Hope from the blanket and into her father's open arms. Hope's little hand reached out for his tie and pulled him down to her level; everyone laughed.

'Just look at her wild black hair!' he said.

Isobel felt a pain in her heart as she looked on. *'It could have been so different. William is missing out on seeing his beautiful child,'* she thought.

Lunch was a great success. Everyone thanked Bo and Ava for such a wonderful spread and, of course, for being such hospitable hosts. When it was time for her parents to leave, Isobel took Hope and handed her to Ava. She needed to say her goodbyes. She walked with them up the drive to their transport as Isobel's mother took her hand.

'You do know that you can come home with Hope any time?'

'Thank you, that means so much to me, but I am happy here Mother. I have my work here now as well, and Ava is teaching me so much about the business. You don't mind, do you?' She didn't want to upset her mother again, not now.

'All I have ever wanted was your happiness, Isobel; I can see you have settled here, and Hope is thriving. We will visit as often as we can, and you can both come and stay with us.'

Isobel kissed them both and waved them off until they disappeared out of the drive. Then, wiping her tears, she walked back to Ava and Hope.

'Are you all right, Isobel?'

'Fine, thank you.'

Sitting in the warm afternoon sun, Ava raised her glass. 'Here's to a happy life for you and Hope.'

'I'll drink to that!'

They say time flies when you're having fun, and in Isobel's case, it was undoubtedly true. Hope was the love she needed in her life, and watching her grow into such a beautiful little girl was a privilege. Ava had cared for them both so well and shown them so much kindness, Isobel knew she would always be indebted to her.

Hope looked upon Ava as a grandmother and loved her like one. Isobel's relationship with her parents blossomed since Hope's birth, and she would visit them regularly, especially when Catherine came to see Ava. She knew the complications it would cause Ava if they did meet and she did not want to break her promise.

Many happy years passed, full of laughter and joy, as Isobel watched Hope grow and flourish.

17

Dust and Feathers

The D'Souza household had settled down with the new baby, and Catherine thanked God every day for her little miracle, Agnes. She was growing into a happy, loving child, and though Catherine spent all day every day with her, when William walked through the door at night, Agnes only had eyes for him.

She was never jealous of their relationship, just happy to see their closeness. Catherine had longed to be a mother for years and had thought of little else.

After waiting fourteen years for Agnes, she had expected motherhood to be everything she had dreamed it would be. But, in reality, she found it very challenging.

William was working long hours again, though he hoped it would be a temporary arrangement. He reminded her daily that he would have to put in the extra hours to keep the house. Catherine agreed, especially now the house had become a natural home for the three of them. Grateful for what they had, Catherine also felt lucky to have her servant girl, Suhani. Thinking back to when Agnes was born, Suhani had been an enormous help – and her mother, of course. William had found Suhani for her, and she had been a loyal and efficient servant girl ever since. In the early days when she struggled, Suhani was always there to help with the baby and was young enough to run after her. Catherine was grateful for all her years of loyal service and she hoped Suhani considered her a friend and not just an employer.

Agnes woke with the sunrise, looked out of her bedroom window and watched the warm Burmese sun, with its orange glow, rise from behind the hills. The chorus of birdsong filled her little ears as she lay back in her bed. Her tummy rumbled, and she ran to her parent's bedroom, eager for her breakfast.

'My little ray of sunshine, we love you dearly, but why so early, Agnes?' William laughed, as he had not long got into bed himself. Lifting her, he held her close to him; they shared a strong bond, one that perhaps Catherine longed for.

'Agnes,' said her mother', time to get dressed now, and then you can start your chores.'

'Yes, Mama,' replied little Agnes.

'You're too hard on the child, Catherine,' said William.

'She has to learn, William, we won't be here forever, and she needs to be able to look after herself.'

'But she is just a child!'

'Nonsense, you are just too soft with her,' replied Catherine sharply.

William knew he was not a great disciplinarian for Agnes; she had him wrapped around her little finger. He thought that Catherine was much better at that sort of task, although Agnes never really gave them a day's trouble.

Her two greatest loves were playing outside, and animals. William and Agnes had tried so hard to persuade Catherine into getting a dog as a pet, to no avail.

'No. You're at work all day, William, and Agnes is at school. I would be the one looking after it: no, thank you.'

However, Catherine conceded, only slightly, and allowed a few chickens – not as pets, she pointed out to Agnes, but as valuable animals to enable them to have fresh eggs every morning. Catherine told her they were to stay in the yard by the kitchen door only, and they were not allowed anywhere near her beautiful garden.

William agreed, he could see the excitement on Agnes's little face, and work began in earnest to build a hen house. The house was painted red, and its roof was black. He constructed a ladder for the hens, and Agnes was thrilled. Together they filled it with straw and headed off to the market to buy some eggs to hatch.

Her new chore for the morning was to check on them. Firstly, she was to make sure they were warm, and turn them very carefully until her father said to stop. William also checked that she had moved them correctly, and would place them with the larger end facing up without her seeing. They then had to be patient and wait for the eggs to hatch. The days ran into three weeks, and then one day Agnes shouted with great excitement, 'The chickens are coming! The chickens are coming!'

William ran outside with Agnes, to witness the great event, and they heard tweeting. In front of them were three tiny balls of yellow fluff. Picking one up gently, Agnes kissed its tiny beak, turning to her father and beaming.

Not staying long as fluffy chicks, they soon grew into busy clucking hens, and now, every morning, her chore was to collect the eggs. Agnes dressed quickly and went straight out to the yard. It was positioned at the back of the house so as to not be in sight for visitors. Catherine's garden was her pride and joy and she had only agreed to have the chickens for their eggs, and to stop the constant pleading from Agnes and William.

Equipped with her bamboo basket, Agnes ran into the yard. The sun was beating down, and as she stood by the hen house, a gust of wind caught the dusty ground, and she shielded her eyes. Running over to the hen house, she opened the small door, and a flurry of feathers came flying out. Then, one by one out stepped her ladies. She knew her mother would scold her if she dawdled, so she hurried them along down the ladder so that she could retrieve the warm eggs. Agnes filled her basket and thanked them all for the treasure, which she did every morning.

'Good morning Lily, good morning Primrose, good morning Buttercup, thank you for my eggs and thank you again.'

Every morning, whilst collecting the eggs, Agnes would sing to the chickens; they enjoyed listening to her whilst laying. Once back in the house, she placed the 'treasure', as she called it, carefully in the larder. Her next chore was to feed them as a reward for all their hard work. She grabbed the bucket of chicken feed and scattered the seed across the yard, calling, 'Here chick-chick-chick, here chick-chick-chick! Come and get it!' There was always a significant skirmish at this moment, and dust and feathers would fly everywhere, adding to Agnes's amusement.

'Agnes! Agnes! What are you doing out there, child?' shouted her mother.

'Nothing, Mama,' giggled Agnes as she walked to the kitchen door.

She was growing fast and was the image of her father, with her wild black hair and deep brown eyes; she was a beautiful little girl.

The day soon arrived for Agnes's first day at school; William had arranged to go into work later so that he and Catherine could take her in together.

Rising even earlier than usual, Agnes was beside herself with excitement. She even managed to get ready herself. Her uniform consisted of a purple checked cotton dress, white ankle socks and black shoes.

Running down to the kitchen, she greeted Suhani, who had prepared her lunch; she quickly put it in her satchel. Then, sitting up at the kitchen table, she only managed to eat a small piece of fruit. After that, she was too excited and ran to the front step and sat down, waiting patiently for her parents to appear.

Agnes was full of energy and eager to get to school and meet her new friends.

William was incredibly proud of his little Agnes, and as they walked hand in hand to the school gate, he knelt beside her and said, 'Remember, Agnes, you're a smart young lady, always work hard and dream big.' Agnes laughed, she didn't understand what he meant. Seeing her sweet little face looking up at him, he tickled her under her chin just like he always did. She kissed her mother and ran into the playground, searching for new friends.

Growing fast, Hope had reached her sixth birthday, and there was great excitement at Sunbird House; she had planned a fashion parade and insisted everyone attend. Isobel, Ava, Bo and Cheng sat on the chairs in the large marble entrance. Hope instructed Ava to play her favourite music on the gramophone. 'The Sunshine one,' she shouted, before dashing to the kitchen where Bo was waiting to help her with the costume changes. 'Are you ready?' she called to Ava, she nodded, and the music began.

Hope made her grand entrance from the kitchen door, draped in Ava's fabric and jewellery. Walking past them towards the staircase, she turned dramatically and returned to the kitchen for a second costume change. After several changes, the show eventually came to a close, to rapturous applause from the audience.

'What a clever little girl you are, Hope. Mummy is so proud of you,' Isobel said, hugging her tightly.

Hope had confided in Ava earlier that day about her plans for the show, but had sworn her to secrecy. Meanwhile, Ava had been arranging a birthday surprise for her for after the show. Kneeling in front of her, Ava took her little hand and said, 'Well, that was an excellent show, Hope, I can see it took a lot of planning, and I always reward hard work – especially as it's your birthday as well.'

She nodded to Cheng, and he disappeared into the kitchen.

Hope was bouncing with excitement, eager to see her reward, as Cheng returned with a large box and placed it carefully onto the floor. Ava watched Hope's face as she rushed to see what was inside it; she stopped abruptly and asked, 'Can I open it, Granny?'

'Of course you can, Hope!' she laughed.

Lifting the lid, Hope let out a delighted squeal and reached into the box. 'Mummy, mummy, it's a puppy!' she shouted. Lifting the squirming puppy out, she struggled to keep hold.

Isobel laughed. 'Put her on the floor, Hope, then she can run about.'

Hope put the puppy down onto the floor and followed her as she bounded towards the kitchen door. Hope ran behind her, and laughter and squeals of joy were heard coming from the garden. Within minutes, the puppy ran around the lobby, with Hope in hot pursuit. Hope ran to Ava and embraced her, saying. 'Thank you, Granny, you're the best.'

Ava, who was thrilled with Hope's reaction, picked her up and sat her on her knee.

'Now, Hope, she will need a lot of love and looking after, but she also needs a name. Can you think of any?'

Hope concentrated hard for a few moments then shouted, 'I know, I know! Can I call her Blossom?'

'Blossom?' replied Ava. 'Well, that's a beautiful name! What made you think of that?'

Thinking hard again, Hope replied. 'You see, Granny, when I am lying in my bed, I can see the trees and the blossom, and it looks so pretty, and I can smell it when the wind blows it to me.

'Mummy, what do you think?' Hope asked Isobel.

'I think Blossom is the perfect name: well done, Hope.'

Blossom had circled the lobby and was bounding towards the kitchen again. Hope tried to catch her, but she was way too fast. Suddenly there was a commotion, and they heard Bo trying to get the dog away from the prepared food on the kitchen table. 'Shoo, Shoo, silly dog!' she called. Blossom had other ideas and dived into the pantry where Bo kept the flour and rice. 'Shoo, Shoo!' she shouted again, as she followed the dog out, flapping the tea towel at her.

Blossom was in full flow now and thought this was an excellent game. She weaved between everyone's legs, covered in flour, from her nose to her tail, leaving a white trail behind her. Ava heard several heated words in Mandarin coming from the kitchen and couldn't help but laugh at the scene unfolding in front of everyone.

By the following day, everyone had calmed down, including Bo, and Hope was so excited to go to school for the first time. Isobel had laid her uniform out on the bed, ready for her to dress, and arranged a special breakfast on the veranda. Once she had eaten, and after telling everyone a hundred times that this was her first day at school, she waved goodbye to them all and walked down the path next to her mother with her small leather satchel on her shoulder.

Arriving at the school gates, Isobel knelt and kissed Hope. 'Now, don't forget your P's and Q's, Hope, and work hard,' she said.

'I will, Mummy,' Hope replied as she skipped happily into the playground.

Catherine's business was expanding, and she had worked so hard to build up her clientele. Now Agnes was in school, allowing her more time to devote to it. Thankfully her mother lived ten houses away down the same street and was always more than happy to have her little granddaughter stay overnight, whenever Catherine's workload was getting too much. Agnes idolised her grandmother, and Catherine could see they had a loving relationship.

If only Catherine's relationship with William were quite so loving. She still loved him, of course: he was the father of her child. When Agnes was born, he had become a changed man, running around to help her with the baby. *Happy times*, she thought.

But now, she could see him slipping back into his old ways; he became distant and preoccupied most of the time, apart from when Agnes needed him. Then, he was the perfect father; he idolised his daughter. It was a shame he didn't feel the same way about his wife. Catherine felt it was all her fault, and took full responsibility for the breakdown in their relationship. Since Agnes was born, their physical relationship had been non-existent: she was always tired, and he worked long hours on his night shift. She thought back to a happier time in Halpin Road and wished they had never moved. Life was simpler then – they had nothing but had everything.

The idea of divorce was abhorrent to her, they had married in the presence of God, and as far as she was concerned, only death could release them.

William had always been a passionate man, she knew that, and to have his conjugal rights withheld must have been difficult for him. Nevertheless, he had convinced her that as long as he had her love, that was all he needed. Somehow, she wasn't confident – perhaps it was the way he said it … whichever way, she felt it lacked sincerity … but was she reading too much into it? He said he loved her, and that was enough for her.

18

A Spider's Web

William's life had changed significantly over the past few years, and his dreams had become reality: a new job, a new house and more money. In addition, William and Catherine had Agnes, the child they had longed for for so many years. But, little by little, William was going back to his old ways. He tried hard to fight it, but 'it is what it is,' as he would say.

He had become intrigued by the servant girl, Suhani, and she had begun to notice his sly glances. She dreamed of leaving service. She was better than that; she deserved more and would stop at nothing to achieve her goals, just like William. She played cat and mouse with him and was very good at the game.

It had all begun a few years back; though no physical contact had occurred between them, the thrill of the chase had kept their tentative relationship alive. Her bedroom door slightly ajar as she changed, knowing William was about to walk past. Lying down on the warm grass on an afternoon off, raising her sari just above her ankles. Bringing him tea on the veranda and gently brushing past him. She knew exactly how to play the game, just like the black widow spider spinning her web, eager for her prey.

One bright early morning, Suhani went into the garden to hang a line of freshly washed sheets. As she reached down to her basket for more pegs, she felt a hand grab her waist from behind and spin her around. It was William. He leant down to kiss her, and she allowed his lips to meet hers for just a few moments, then pulled away. Pushing him away, she smoothed her dress down and said, 'Mr D'Souza, what do you think you are doing?'

William looked embarrassed; had he read the signals wrong? 'I am so sorry. I thought you ...'

'You thought what, Mr D'Souza?' she replied, smiling at him. She then leant in and kissed him passionately behind the screen of the hanging sheets.

Picking up her basket, she walked swiftly towards the kitchen with her head held high, smiling to herself. William wanted her even more now and watched with longing as she walked away.

Suhani needed patience if she wanted to become the next Mrs D'Souza, and her relationship with William, however complex, was worth the wait. They met several times a week, either in the room at York Road or their secret place by The Royal Lake. William tried to take their relationship further than kisses and caresses. Still, she didn't allow him any more, controlling the situation with a sultry smile and a promise of more to come.

She remembered the first time she had met him. She was buying some vegetables and fish to cook for herself and her mother. Sensing someone was watching, she turned and saw William. He smiled and walked towards her. She thought how handsome he was, with his wild black hair and dark eyes. They began to talk, nothing of any consequence initially, but within that conversation, William had asked if she would like to come and work for him. It was an offer she could not refuse. He explained that the position was to help his pregnant wife run the house. It wasn't what Suhani was expecting, but she was desperate for money as she had been living off the pittance her mother earned. She accepted, and William gave her the address, explaining that his wife would, of course, make the final decision. He then arranged a day and time when they would both be at the house.

'I look forward to seeing you again; sorry, I didn't catch your name?' he asked as he held out his hand.

'Suhani, my name is Suhani.'

As he took her hand in his, she blushed and felt her heart race. Moving closer to him, she could feel his breath on her face. People began to stare at them, so she pulled away.

'Don't be late!' he laughed as he disappeared into the crowd.

Suhani had stood there for a few moments, still flushed; he intrigued her and she looked forward to seeing him again.

And now, all these years later, she had him exactly where she wanted him. She had watched the slow decline of his marriage and almost felt sorry for his poor deluded wife. Why hadn't Catherine suspected him? Perhaps she did know but chose to ignore it all. Suhani would continue to play the seductress to secure her place with William; the D'Souza's would divorce and she would become the new Mrs D'Souza. There was just one more obstacle to overcome in her plan, and that was his child, Agnes; she was a sweet girl and Suhani had grown fond of her.

She had overheard an argument between William and his wife concerning Agnes. Mrs D'Souza had told William of her plan to send Agnes away to school when she reached eight years old, and William was having none of it.

'You cannot send her away! She is far too young, Catherine,' he shouted.

'I have spoken to Father O'Brian at St Mary's; it is all arranged, William. When Agnes is eight, the Sisters will take her as a boarder.'

The argument had continued long into the evening, and Suhani had heard enough to make her smile; she merely needed to bide her time and be patient.

Knowing that their marriage was having problems, Suhani was happy to offer William some comfort; it was the least she could do.

The thought of having to wait two more long years of secrecy and lies was too much for Suhani to contemplate and the time was fast approaching for a request. Her need to become the lady of the house was growing and becoming overpowering. She hated being the poor little servant girl who slept in the room by the kitchen door.

It was her time to wear the crown.

Suhani knew how much William adored her, and after spending several nights together at York Road, she had him in the palm of her hand. He promised her the world during their wild moments of passion, telling her over and over how one day they would be together. But was William being truthful? Or were they empty promises? Suhani was still young, unlike William, now middle-aged; he was lucky to have her.

Today was the day she decided William had to make his choice. The sun was shining, and a warm breeze swept gently through her long silky hair. Breathing in the sweet smell of the Rangoon honeysuckle, she carried the wicker basket laden with freshly washed laundry into the garden. Whilst hanging the sheets on the line, William surprised her from behind the washing line, grabbing her around the waist and kissing the nape of her neck. She allowed his hands to move down her body and over her curves, then she held his hand.

'I need you to do something for me,' she said.

'Anything for you, my darling,' he replied, continuing to kiss her neck.

'Anything?' she asked.

'Yes, of course, Suhani, you know I would do anything for you.'

'William, do you know how much I love you?'

'I know you love me, Suhani.'

'If you will do anything for me, then I want you to tell Catherine about us.'

He pulled away. 'Why today? Aren't we happy the way we are?'

'No, William, I am not happy like this. I want us to have a normal life together; I want to be your wife, not your skivvy! I think you owe me that at least!'

'It's not that easy – I have Agnes to consider.'

'When we are together properly, we can have children of our own, William, and live as a normal family. Agnes can come and stay with us.

'It needs to be said today, William. I have the rest of the day off, so I am going to York Road to prepare our celebratory meal, and once you have told Catherine, please make your way there. I will be waiting. I know Catherine is going to Maria's with Agnes today, so you will have to speak to her before she goes. You don't need to tell Agnes anything about us yet – leave that for another day.'

The colour drained from William's face. He hadn't been expecting this and she could see he wasn't happy with her demands, so she continued. 'Well, William, let me put it another way to make it simpler for you to understand: Either you tell Catherine, or I will – and knowing what a wonderful husband you have been to her, I am sure you would rather she heard this from you.'

Picking up her basket, Suhani began to make her way under the sheets and back to the kitchen. William followed her and, just before she went through the door, she turned to him and said, 'I will be at York Road and your meal will be ready at ten o'clock sharp; don't be late.'

Placing her basket on the table, still being watched by William, she took off her housecoat, grabbed her bag and made her way to the front door. As she opened the door, she blew him a kiss and left.

William stood there for a few moments, his mind whirling. Suhani had given him an ultimatum; was he now seeing her true colours?

That money-grabbing, manipulative bitch! What can I do? As he paced the floor like a trapped animal with no escape route. How could he speak to Catherine and tell her he was leaving? Suhani had been fun, but never a replacement for Catherine. With so many thoughts running through his mind, he didn't see Agnes coming down the stairs.

'Daddy, Daddy!' she shouted, running towards him. William scooped her up in his arms. 'I am going to Grandma's, Daddy, and I am allowed to sleep there *all night*!' she said excitedly.

'Are you now? Well, I will miss my little poppet,' he replied, tickling her, as she put her arms around his neck.

'I love you, Daddy,' she said, holding him tight.

'I love you too, my darling Agnes.' William kissed her little cheeks. 'Now be a good girl for your Grandma, and I will see you tomorrow.'

'Yes, Daddy, I'll be good.'

Catherine walked down the stairs. 'I won't be here tonight either William, has Agnes told you …?'

'No, she said she is going to your mother's for the night.'

'Mother could do with some company, so I will stay there.'

'I will see you tomorrow then,' he replied.

How had their marriage become so cold and Catherine become so distant? he thought.

Agnes was eager to see Grandma, but she turned and ran back to William as they walked towards the door.

'Love you again, Daddy,' she said, kissing him on his cheek.

'Love you too, Agnes,' he said, and he watched them leave the house.

'How could I possibly break up my family?' he thought.

'If only I had paid my wife more attention, rather than looking elsewhere. Perhaps if I had, then I wouldn't be standing in this entrance lobby having to make a life-changing decision.'

19

The Dying Flames of Passion

Walking into the dining room, William poured himself a double whisky from the drinks cabinet. Swigging it back in one, he pushed the bottle into the inside pocket of his jacket and left the house.

It was a beautiful day, and the streets were busy with people rushing to be somewhere else. He walked for a while, deep in thought, only stopping for another drink. Then, looking up, he soon realised he had walked to his magnificent Shwedagon Pagoda; he breathed in deeply and asked for some divine guidance to get him out of this mess.

Sitting down on the grass, he lit a cigarette and slowly inhaled the smoke. He sat there until darkness came and his bottle was empty. Then, getting up slowly, he made his way across the streets to the market and, after buying himself another bottle, took a slug.

'She can't tell me what to do! Who does she think she is? I'll show her who's in charge!' he shouted as people passed him, staring.

'What are you staring at?' he shouted.

The whisky had given him courage, and he continued to fight his way through the crowded market until he found his favourite bar and staggered in.

Sitting down abruptly, he tried to appear sober. 'Barman, double whisky – now!'

A young Thai waitress collected his drink from the bar and placed it on her tray. She walked over to William and carefully put it down on the table in front of him. Fumbling in his pocket, he pulled out some notes, leant over, grabbed her wrist and pulled her into his lap.

As he tried to kiss her, she pushed him away.

'There's no need to be like that,' he said, attempting to kiss her again.

Suddenly the waitress was lifted off his lap by the sizeable Chinese barman. He wore a sweat-stained vest, and a stubby unlit cigar hung from his mouth. Staring at William, he tapped a sharp machete on the table, shouting in a menacing voice, 'Do not want trouble; you go now!'

William knew it was time to leave; he threw money on the table and staggered out onto the dark streets. He continued zigzagging through the streets and dodged traffic coming at him from all directions. Wanting a quiet place to sit, he eventually found a spot by the side of the road and, leaning up against a tree, bit the cork from his second bottle of whisky, spitting it out onto the street. After taking a drink from the bottle, he wiped his mouth with the back of his sleeve and fumbled in his pocket for his cigarettes and matches. He managed to light the match but then dropped it onto his trousers. The smell of burning fabric woke him from his drunken stupor, and he frantically hit his trouser leg until extinguished. Needing more drink, he took a long slow slug of whisky, stood up slowly and began walking home.

Zig-zagging across the street he suddenly fell onto the ground in front of a passing rickshaw. The driver stopped abruptly, his passenger thrown back into the cab, the driver shouted at William to get out of the way. William managed to rise to his feet slowly; whilst trying to remain upright, he roughly brushed the dust from his trousers and cursed the driver.

The passenger looked on in shock, keeping back in the shadow of the cab, not wanting to be recognised. She watched as he meandered across the street till eventually out of sight.

'Follow him,' she told the driver,'but keep your distance, I don't want him to see us.'

They slowly continued and then turned into William and Catherine's street, stopping at the corner. 'Wait here for me,' she told the driver and stepped down from the cab. Ava continued to walk down the street to the house and looked up at the windows, but it was in darkness.

That's strange, she thought, *Catherine's light in her workroom is normally on at this time, she always works late.* She waited a while, just to see if there were any signs of life at the house.

Meanwhile, William arrived at the kitchen door and, finding it locked and unable to find his key, pushed it hard with his body and fell into the kitchen. 'Ssh! Sssh!' he told himself and laughed, he had a vague recollection of being told he would be alone tonight. He continued to fumble his way into the dining room and, finding the drinks cabinet open, he grabbed the large bottle of whisky off the shelf.

'Perfect,' he said.

William saw the small gas lamp on the table and, still swaying from the alcohol, grabbed the matches and lit it, after several failed attempts. Gripping the lamp in one hand and his shoes in the other, he staggered towards the stairs. He eventually reached the top and put the lamp down on the landing, steadying himself. After rearranging the shoes and whisky in his hands, he picked up the lamp again. Still swaying, he made his way along the landing and fell into a room, the gas lamp slipping from his hand.

'Damn,' he said as he watched a small piece of rug catch fire. Using his shoe, he extinguished the small smouldering mass.

He found himself in Catherine's workroom by mistake but was too drunk to care. He could see plenty of rolls of soft fabric to lie on and found a corner in which to settle down, near the adjoining door to their bedroom. With drink still on his mind, he pulled the cork of the new bottle out with his teeth, spat it across the room, and lifted the bottle to his mouth, taking another long slug. Struggling to light a cigarette, he eventually put it in his mouth and inhaled deeply.

Slumped down, William grabbed a pile of fabric and pushed it behind him. With one hand on the bottle of whisky, and the lit cigarette held loosely between in the other, he drifted off into a drunken sleep.

Ava had waited long enough and felt a panic rise in her. 'Oh my, what if he has hurt Catherine, and she is laying defenceless against that drunken monster!' Her heart racing, she ran to the back of the house and through the garden to the kitchen door. She reached for the handle and pushed it gently, it was open. The house was in darkness apart from the soft glow of moonlight in the hallway from the atrium above. It was just enough for her to see her way up the staircase and as she reached the top she noticed the glow of a gas lamp coming from Catherine's room.

'She must be here,' she thought, and continued down the landing to her door, putting her ear to it and listening for the sound of a sewing machine. She knocked but there was no response, so she slowly opened the door. She saw the oil lamp on the floor and, as she picked it up, made the shocking discovery of William propped up by the rolls of fabric. He was hunched in a drunken stupor in the corner of the room by the adjoining doors. She stepped back in fright, her heart pounding fast, she needed to leave but was also desperate to find Catherine. Moving slowly towards him, her hands shaking as she carried the oil lamp, she stood as close as she felt safe to him and asked, 'Where is Catherine?'

There was no reply. 'Where is Catherine?' she repeated, but still no reply. She edged closer and raised her voice. 'What have you done with my Catherine?' she shouted.

William began to mumble something inaudible. 'Speak up William, where is Catherine?' This was his last chance.

'Maria, Agnes,' he muttered. 'Gone ...' and the words petered out to nothing. What a sorrowful sight he was, Ava might have felt pity for him if she didn't hate him so much. Relieved that Catherine was safe at her mother's house with Agnes, she was about to leave when she noticed a lit cigarette ready to drop from William's fingers. She could have left it there with the possibility of him setting himself on fire with the aid of the spilt whisky, or she could remove it: what a dilemma! Ava thought of Agnes without a father and knew she couldn't have that on her conscience, so decided to remove it. Placing the gas lamp on the floor by William's leg, she leant over and began to carefully remove the cigarette from his fingers; frightened of waking him, she slowly pulled away. Suddenly he grabbed her wrist and instinctively she pulled away releasing his hold and staggered back in horror. She ran for the door but the hem of her skirt knocked the oil lamp over. Without realising and desperate to escape, she ran through the open door, slamming it behind her. She went as fast as she could down the stairs and out to the waiting cab. Once inside she told the driver to take her home as quickly as possible. The driver looked at her suspiciously as she tried to catch her breath, her body visibly shaken by the ordeal, but he said nothing and began the journey back.

Earlier that day, Catherine had told William she was going to stay at her mother's house, but as she walked along she had begun to feel guilty and changed her mind. Her orders were growing and she really couldn't afford to have an evening off. Agnes would be fine on her own, she loved her grandmother and was very excited to be staying overnight. As they walked along the street, Agnes saw her best friend Nilar carrying fruit with her mother to the market. They waved and smiled, and she skipped the last few yards to her grandma's door.

Maria, Catherine's mother, had lived alone in the house for the past two years after losing her husband Michael. Catherine remembered the day she had told her parents about William's promotion and their new house; they were thrilled for them. especially as they would now be closer.

Maria had watched Agnes grow from a baby into a fun-loving, happy six-year-old. She loved having her over; they shared a beautiful relationship, and Agnes loved her dearly.

Once Catherine had explained to her mother, she left Agnes and returned home to continue with her orders. To have a whole free day was a luxury, and she didn't want to waste a minute.

After several hours had passed, she went downstairs to the kitchen. It was almost dark. *Goodness, whatever is the time?* she said to herself.

'Hello?' she called out, waiting for Suhani to answer, but there was no reply.

That's strange, she thought.

She lit the gas lamp, threw a log into the range, and gradually the kitchen became illuminated with a warm glow. Stirring a pot of green curry, she placed it on the hotplate and the room soon filled with a delicious aroma. As she sat down, Catherine began to think of her darling little Agnes; she was so lucky to have such a sweet child and felt relaxed knowing how much she loved to stay at her Grandma's.

Once Catherine had finished her meal, she picked up the lamp and walked into the dining room. The drinks cabinet was open, and Catherine noticed two bottles were missing from the top shelf. Perhaps she was mistaken? She would ask Suhani in the morning.

Browsing through the selection, she eventually decided on a small glass of sherry. Catherine never was a big drinker, but a little glass of sherry wouldn't hurt. Carrying the tray with the half bottle of sherry and glass, Catherine walked up the stairs to her bedroom, went in and closed the door.

Suhani had spent most of her day preparing the room at York Road, and knowing how wretched the room looked, she had her work cut out, trying to transform it into something resembling stylish. She needed something to brighten the room and, luckily for her, saw a large shop on the corner selling fabric. In the window was a roll of red chiffon.

'Perfect,' she thought, and entered the shop. After asking the shopgirl for six yards of the material the girl placed the roll of fabric on the table and began to cut. Making small talk, the assistant asked Suhani if she was planning to make anything nice with it.

'Yes, I am going to make a tablecloth – it's for tonight. My … er … *boyfriend* is going to ask me to marry him tonight, and I wanted to make the place look extra special.'

'Goodness!' the shop girl replied. 'You must be very certain he will ask you if you're going to all this trouble.'

'Oh yes, I am very certain. We had a conversation just this morning about it, and he knows I am expecting him to ask me.'

'How exciting for you! I do hope all goes well for you both,' she said, handing Suhani the fabric. 'If you need anything else for your special evening, I will be happy to help.'

'Thank you, that's very kind of you, and your name is?' Suhani inquired.

'My name is Isobel, and I will be here all day till six o'clock.'

'Thank you, Isobel,' replied Suhani, and she left the shop.

Once in the room, she set about cleaning it, adding a few extra touches by knocking a couple of nails into the far walls and hanging two pictures. One of them was a painting of a young Indian girl dressed in a beautiful sari. Suhani thought William would see the similarity to her. The second picture was of a small house nestled in a beautiful garden; this was her dream, one she wanted to share with William.

Knocking in the last nail, she hung a small ornate gold clock with black hands, on the wall by the door. The clock had been one of the few items her family had managed to bring from their home in India. She had kept it safe in her room at the D'Souzas for all these years, and now it took pride of place. It made a loud ticking noise, but she didn't mind: it brought back memories from back home. It had hung in the main room where all the family would eat together. She missed those special times – life was not the same now.

Unrolling the red chiffon fabric, Suhani spread it across the table, placing two plates and two glasses on top. Then, looking around the room, she took her candles and put one on the old cupboard and two by the window.

Now it was time to prepare herself for the memorable evening ahead. Suhani, naturally, needed to look extra fabulous for William tonight. So the evening's preparations began with her long slender legs, as she opened a jar of coconut oil and, starting with her ankles, smoothed the oil over her skin, continuing to the top of her thighs. Lifting her tiny bottle of cologne, she dabbed some behind her ears and onto her cleavage. She then slipped into her red silk sari, with golden thread that glistened in the candlelight.

Looking in the mirror by the door, she checked her lipstick, a deep blood red full lip. *How could he resist me?* she thought, laughing to herself.

Brushing her smooth, long black hair, she allowed it to fall just in front of the low neckline; as the evening progressed, she planned to flick her hair back, revealing a glimpse of her cleavage. Moving to the bed, she sprinkled a little ginseng and ylang-ylang essential oils; she had been told by an old practitioner in the town that these had great aphrodisiac qualities – not that she needed it, but she was leaving nothing to chance.

Suhani's preparation for a perfect meal was complete. At nine forty-five precisely, the food would finish being cooked by her Burmese friend, Hlaing, who had orders to bring it directly to her. She looked at the clock: it was already nine forty-five – the time had flown by – and Hlaing was running up the stairs shouting. Suhani could now begin to lay the feast on the table, ready in anticipation for William.

Once everything was in place, Suhani sat down on the chair facing the door, swept her hair to fall in front of her shoulder and licked her lips. She was expecting William at any minute, a meeting that would change her life forever. She was ready.

Tick-tock, went the clock.

Agnes ran into her grandma's arms; she was so excited to be staying the night.

Earlier, Maria had set up a little bed beside her own, and once it was nightfall, Agnes kneeled by her bed and said her prayers. 'God bless Mummy, God bless Daddy, and God bless Grandma … oh, and if you would be so kind, please bless my chickens, especially Buttercup as she has a poorly leg, thank you, God, Amen.' She then hopped into bed and was soon fast asleep.

A little while later, Agnes was awakened by the sound of voices. She wasn't sure at first if she was awake, or still dreaming. Rubbing her eyes, she got out of bed and followed the noise; she could hear her grandmother's voice. 'What is it, Grandma? What's all that noise?'

'There is a fire down the road, Agnes– they think it's Mrs Singh's house.'

Agnes rubbed her eyes again and pushed gently past her grandma to get a better view. The dark street was illuminated by the glow of the roaring flames, and Agnes saw lots of men shouting and running back and forth to the well.

'Faster, faster!' shouted one man, holding a bucket of water and running past their doorway. 'Get the fire pump quickly: there are people in that house!' he yelled. Several men began to push a large cart as hard as they could towards the small river by the houses, and Agnes saw the giant metal pump with a long hose attached to it.

There was so much confusion in the streets, with soot-covered men carrying heavy buckets of water past them towards the fire.

Tick-tock.

Catherine wondered briefly about William's whereabouts, but she knew he would come home eventually, even if only to see Agnes.

She had fallen asleep quickly that night; she usually struggled and would lie awake for hours. But not tonight – after having several glasses of sherry, slumber became much more accessible. She dreamt of William on their wedding day. That twinkle in his eyes, sweeping her up in his arms and holding her tight. Round and round, they glided over the dancefloor, with everyone else invisible to them, and his deep brown eyes looking at her full of love and promise. She smiled in her sleep and hugged her pillow.

Tick-tock.

Suhani was still sitting on the chair and looking at the door, and every time she heard a noise she would straighten up and flick her hair in anticipation, only to be disappointed again.

Looking across at the clock and seeing it was now ten-thirty, she wasn't too concerned. William was not a great timekeeper; he had probably become distracted and was now on his way.

Tick-tock.

By now, the whole street was outside: women holding their hands to their mouths in shock, children crying, and husbands running towards the fire in a vain attempt to extinguish it.

Agnes could feel the warmth on her face from the fire and moved a little further onto the street.

'Stay close, Agnes,' said her grandma, 'it's not safe.'

But Agnes managed to wriggle from her grandma's hand and ran to the middle of the road.

Tick-tock.

Suhani opened the door and stood at the top of the staircase; she looked across the courtyard, hoping to catch a glimpse of William. She knew he loved her. Of course he loved her.

Perhaps she had been too sharp with him in the garden? He *had* looked very shocked by her request.

He has had the whole day to tell Catherine he is leaving her! What is keeping him?

Going back into the room, Suhani started to pace the floor. *What if he's changed his mind? He could be in her arms right now! They could be trying to make their marriage work. I bet he hasn't even told Catherine about me, but he belongs to me. I have been his mistress for six long years. I will not let him make a fool out of me.*

Suhani looked at the clock again. It was now eleven o'clock. Where the hell was he? *Surely he wouldn't let me down, would he? His love for me is more than he ever felt for his wife; he has whispered those very words to me a hundred times and said he adores me.*

She thought about all of their nights of passion, nights where she had left him breathless and wanting more.

She looked at the clock again: it was now eleven-thirty.

Convincing herself that he hadn't been brave enough to tell his wife, she could feel the anger rising; she wrung her hands and continued to pace the floor. *I will give him just thirty more minutes*, she thought, *but he had better show his face soon.*

Tick-tock.

William's hand relaxed as the bottle of whisky poured out its contents onto him and the surrounding fabric.

Having drunk himself into a stupor, he remained unconscious and oblivious to his fate. The oil lamp's flame had ignited the whisky-soaked fabric, and within minutes the thick black smoke enveloped him where he lay. The flame ran along the length of the rug, setting light to the base of the fabric rolls standing against the wall. The fire soon took hold and travelled quickly up towards the ceiling as the choking black smoke found the gap under the adjoining door.

Tick-tock.

Whilst the thick black smoke crept silently under the door and rolled along the floor, rising and falling in small waves, Catherine slept.

Its long twisted finger reached out across the room, outstretched towards her, getting closer.

Tick-tock.

Suhani picked up a plate from the table and threw it against the wall, soon followed by the glasses. Grabbing the tablecloth, she pulled the feast onto the floor. Her rage was growing fierce from the pit of her stomach,

'How dare he?' she screamed, looking at the clock again. It was now midnight. Enough was enough. Running down the stairs, she made her way through the crowds in the market to the top of William's Street.

As she turned the corner, she saw flames and smoke billowing from the roof of William's house. Men ran past her with buckets of water, shouting to one another to get more. Two soot-covered men pointed a large hose towards the house whilst another pushed frantically down on a pump, forcing the river's water into the hose. Passing them, she ran to the house and into the hallway. Thick black smoke filled the air.

Running into the kitchen, she grabbed the cloth from the draining board, ran it under the tap, and tied it around her face. Then she ran back into the hallway and began to climb the marble staircase, but the air was so thick with the rancid hot smoke that she became disoriented and fell to her knees.

Crawling along the landing, Suhani made her way to William and Catherine's bedroom, screaming his name – 'William, William! Fire!' – but there was no response. Continuing to crawl through the smoke, she reached up and grabbed a door handle. It was uncomfortably hot to the touch and she withdrew her hand quickly.

Ripping her sari, she placed the fabric on the handle and pushed the door open. As it opened, a vast fireball rolled across the ceiling and through the open door; she threw herself onto the floor. The room was an inferno, with flames lapping every corner. Quickly realising this was Catherine's workroom and not her and William's bedroom, she crawled along the landing to the next room. The smoke and heat were intense and Suhani knew time was running out and they would perish if she didn't get out of there soon. She turned around on the floor, positioning her feet towards the door and kicked it with all her might. A vast billowing cloud of blackness escaped through the door as it broke open; her lungs heavy with smoke and her eyes now blind in the darkness, she could only feel her way to the bed. She called out William's name but heard no reply.

'William! William!' Suhani screamed again, but there was no response and she could hear the loud noise of the fire engulfing the room next door. Time was running out.

Tick-tock.

Agnes froze. She couldn't see much of the house, only the enormous red and yellow flames, fighting to reach the sky whilst lapping at the building. The vast clouds of black billowing smoke immersed the street with its darkness.

'No!' screamed Agnes. 'No, Grandma! It's my house!' Agnes turned and ran towards the inferno.

'Agnes, Stop! Stop!' Maria tried to grab her little hand, but she was too quick. 'Stop her, please, somebody!' Maria screamed.

Agnes ran faster than she had ever run before, tears streaming down her face. 'Daddy! Daddy!!' she screamed.

As she reached the end of the street, the intense heat stopped her from going any further. Chaos surrounded her. Men ran past with buckets of water, desperately trying to extinguish the fire, women screaming at them to help the people trapped inside.

Tick-tock.

Grabbing the person's arms, Suhani managed to pull them off the bed and dragged them out of the room towards the stairs. Not knowing if it was William or Catherine, in the panic, looking down through the thick black smoke she felt the face. It was Catherine.

Hearing a strange noise, she looked up; a ball of flame from the workroom had taken hold of the landing carpet and was travelling fast towards her. In that split second, she made a decision.

Live or die? she thought, *you or me?*

She dragged Catherine's unconscious body down the flight of stairs, a feat that took all of Suhani's strength. As they reached the entrance hall, she looked up to where they had just been. The ceiling had collapsed, debris piled high on the bed, and fire engulfed the room. Suhani continued to drag Catherine out through the front door until she reached the safety of the lawn. Exhausted, she removed the cloth from her face and knelt beside Catherine, shaking her to wake up; she hadn't risked her own life for her to die.

'Wake up! Wake up!'

Several minutes passed, with Suhani still looking down at Catherine.

Was it so wrong to wish her dead? On the contrary, it would make my life easier, she thought. *Thank goodness William wasn't in the house, but he has a lot of explaining to do when I see him next.*

Catherine coughed and opened her eyes, her face black with soot; she reached out her hand.

Tick. Tock. STOP.

Time stood still for Agnes that night. She was looking beyond the fire; she couldn't see the flames or the smoke, she couldn't hear the crying or the screaming. All she could see was her father smiling back at her.

As she stood there, her face red from the glow of the flames, she felt someone touch her shoulder and turned around. It was her grandmother.

Agnes stared anxiously at her, waiting for her to say everything was all right.

'Help! Help! Can somebody help us, please?' cried Suhani.

Agnes and Maria heard the shouting coming from the garden.

'Quick, Grandma, I can hear someone,' Agnes cried, running through the gate. As they reached the garden, they saw two people on the grass. 'Mummy!' screamed Agnes as she threw herself at Catherine.

'Oh, my darling child,' Catherine cried, hugging her tight.

'The fire, Mummy, the fire! Is Daddy with you? Where is he?' Agnes looked desperately around the garden.

'Daddy isn't here, Agnes …'

Without giving her mother the chance to continue, Agnes cried, 'Daddy is in the fire, help him, Mummy, help him!' Maria tried to comfort her, but she was too distraught.

Catherine reached for her mother's hand, saying quietly, 'Mother, he didn't come home last night; it was late when I went to my bed, and he still wasn't home. So where is he when I need him?'

Suhani was thinking the same.

Maria helped her daughter up and, holding Agnes's hand together with Suhani, walked past the house and down the drive. Agnes looked back at her home in tears.

As they reached the street, a large hose was still pumping gallons of water onto the roof. Finally, the fire was under control.

Covered in soot and exhausted, the four of them slowly walked to Maria's house. Once indoors, Maria took Agnes off to bed and then the three women sat at the kitchen table in silence. They had all shared the same nightmare.

Catherine broke the silence. Looking at Suhani, her dress ripped and her body black from the smoke and ash, she held her hand out to her and said, 'You saved my life; how can I ever repay you, even risking your own life for me?' Pushing the chair away, she leant over and put her arms around Suhani's shoulders and sobbed.

'You are so brave, thank you for saving my daughter. If there is anything I can do for you, *anything*, please tell me!' cried Maria.

'I am not brave. Anyone would have done the same in the circumstances. Thank you for your kind words, but they're not necessary,' Suhani replied, feeling embarrassed and ashamed.

Maria made a pot of tea and placed a bottle of brandy on the table next to it. After their horrific ordeal, hot tea and a spot of brandy were in order.

Suhani and Catherine had to share the guest bedroom and, after trying to wash as much soot off their bodies as they could, they collapsed, exhausted into the bed.

The moon was shining bright and filled the room; Catherine was soon asleep, but Suhani lay there awake until morning. There were too many issues to resolve in her head before she could sleep again.

20

The Aftermath

Once the sun had risen, Suhani gently slid from the bed and silently made her way out of the house and back up the street to the D'Souza's house. The smell of burning embers was still thick in the air and debris from the roof scattered the street.

Walking to the back of the house, she could see that the kitchen door was open and she carefully entered. The ceilings, walls and windows were covered in thick black soot, and indistinguishable objects were hidden under a thick black film.

Slowly stepping into the entrance lobby, she noticed the front door was ajar; she then remembered kicking it open when trying to escape last night. The ornate marble floor and staircase were black and wet underfoot and water still dripped from the large gaping holes in the roof. Everywhere had the smell of a spent fire, and it stuck to the back of her throat.

The fire damage was minimal downstairs, but it had not escaped the smoke damage. The furniture still intact was utterly black.

Lifting a box of matches from the table, Suhani began to investigate, looking for clues as to how the fire started.

She noticed the oil lamp was missing from the centre of the table, and she saw three spent matches.

She knew Mrs D'Souza wouldn't have moved it, so where had it gone? The only other person was William. Was he the one who took the oil lamp? She also noticed that the drinks cabinet was open. There were two gaps on the top shelf, and one from the bottom, though she remembered stocking it up only the other day with two large bottles of whisky and a small bottle of sherry, all three now missing.

Catherine never drinks – perhaps the odd sherry, but never hard spirits. So why would she have taken it? That doesn't make any sense, thought Suhani, concluding that it must have been William. *He lit the lamp threw the spent matches onto the table and took the bottles of whiskey. He was probably drunk, she thought.*

Carefully stepping across the large puddles on the marble floor, she eventually reached the handrail and pulled herself up onto the first step of the stairs. Daylight was peeking through the broken timbers of the wooden roof above, and waves of black soot covered every corner of the stairs – as if a sea of smoke had risen, then receded, leaving its mark before disappearing. The pungent smell of damp, wet wood hung in the air, and trying not to slip was difficult enough without trying to avoid the dripping water from the sodden rooftop.

As Suhani reached the top of the staircase, she saw the true devastation caused by the fire.

Placing her feet carefully in the spaces between the fallen timbers from above, she entered the bedroom. She shivered and felt a chill down her spine. Then, suddenly, she had a flashback: she had pulled Catherine off the bed and was dragging her body onto the landing. The fire was reaching down for her at speed.

Steadying herself, she took a deep breath and went through to the bedroom. The adjoining door hung precariously and, after climbing over the fallen roof timbers, she had to move it carefully to get into Catherine's workroom. Stepping over the debris that now littered the floor from the damaged ceiling, Suhani took a long slow look around the room. It was the most damaged room in the house, with every wall burnt through, and the thick smell of charred wood lingered in her nostrils. Water was still running down the walls from the now open space – once the roof – and what used to be fabric rolls were now charred sticks propped up against the wall.

The fire must have started in here, but how? she thought.

As she walked through the room, burnt remnants of fabric stuck to her shoes, and as she tried to kick them off, she caught her foot on something hard. Looking down, she picked it up, brushed off the soot, and saw that it was the base of the gas lamp. Perhaps Catherine had forgotten about it and placed it too close to the fabrics?

Suhani began to scour the floor for clues and circled the room, eventually ending at the adjoining door. She tripped and fell to the floor, and as she pushed herself up, she felt something by her hand. She glanced to see what it was and froze, too frightened to look again. Then, praying it wasn't what she thought it was, she forced herself to take another look. Standing up slowly, she moved closer. Sticking out from under the pile of timber was a soot-covered shoe, a man's shoe. She began to remove the wood, plank by plank, fearing what she was about to reveal.

As she neared the bottom, she was tentatively reaching out for the last plank when she heard her name called. She spun around to see Catherine standing in the room.

'Whatever are you doing?' she shouted.

'I think I have found the cause of the fire,' Suhani replied calmly, looking down.

'What do you mean?' Moving to where Suhani was standing, Catherine looked down at the pile of timbers, and her gaze immediately fell onto the shoe. As she staggered back in fright, Suhani reached out and grabbed her hand.

'I have to remove the last piece of wood, Catherine, then we will know,' she said. Catherine nodded frantically, and Suhani leant down and slowly lifted the last piece.

Screams echoed around the house and out onto the street.

Ava rushed to Maria's after hearing about the fire and as they sat around the kitchen a feeling of disbelief and grief circled them all. She held Catherine's hand and asked, 'How did it happen?'

Catherine remained silent, her life as she knew it had been snatched away from her and she had no words to describe the pain in her heart. Maria nodded to Ava to leave Catherine a moment as she needed to speak to her.

They walked into the garden and sat down on the wicker seats, shaded by a large umbrella. 'Was there anyone else in the house, Maria?' Ava asked, knowing only too well she had left William in there.

'Unfortunately, yes Ava, there was,' Maria replied. 'It was William and he didn't survive.'

Ava was in shock, how could he be dead? He was very drunk and needed to sleep it off – but dead? She had removed the cigarette from his hand, even though he frightened her half to death. She didn't understand but she soon realised that she must have been the last person to see him alive.

Maria continued, 'Catherine is very lucky to be alive … if it wasn't for Suhani ...' She stopped talking and reached for her handkerchief. Ava stood up and put her arms around Maria and felt her sobbing on her shoulder. Once she had composed herself she continued, 'Suhani dragged my daughter out of bed and down the stairs to the garden just before the ceiling collapsed and the bedroom became an inferno. She saved her life.'

'Poor Catherine … but I thought Catherine was staying at yours last night with Agnes?

'She was going to stay but changed her mind at the last moment; you know Catherine, always worrying about her work. How did you know, Ava, it was all last minute?'

'Oh, I think she may have mentioned it in passing that she had so much work on she might have to postpone her stay with you.' Maria nodded in acceptance of her answer.

'And they said it was definitely William in the fire?' Ava asked.

'Yes, it was definitely him, although as you can imagine he was unrecognisable. They found his wedding ring amongst the ashes and it had the inscription to Catherine inside. The fireman thinks he must have knocked the oil lamp over and, what with the whisky on his clothes, well … it doesn't bear thinking about.'

Ava looked at Maria in disbelief. But when she ran out of the room, the oil lamp was by his leg … or was it? Had she caused William's death and taken a father away from his child?

'I don't know what to say, Maria. I am so sorry, your daughter has lost her husband and your granddaughter has lost her father. If there is anything I can do, please ask.'

They returned to the kitchen; Catherine hadn't moved from her seat, still with a look of total loss on her face. Suddenly she said, 'What was he doing in my room, why hadn't he just gone to bed? They found a large bottle of whisky, he must have been drinking heavily all day to have collapsed in the room. I just don't understand: he never drank! We'd spoken yesterday morning, Agnes was telling him about going to see Grandma, and they hugged and … well … you know how much they adored each other.'

'Have you had a chance to speak to her yet?' Ava asked.

'No, I just can't find the words. I will be the one responsible for breaking her heart, Ava, how can I do that?'

Catherine's eyes were red and swollen from all the tears she had shed since William's death. She hadn't slept for more than a few hours each night since the fire, the nightmare still fresh in her mind. As she lay in her bed, still wide awake, the image of William laying there amongst the debris of the fire was almost too much to bear.

'Everything is dark, Ava. I am standing still, yet all around me life continues. I want to scream and shout and say, 'Stop laughing! Stop getting on with your life! He is dead; my life has stopped.'

As Ava put her arms around Catherine to comfort her and let her cry, she had to turn her head away. Was she responsible for breaking her heart? They sat in Maria's kitchen, holding each other, allowing the tears to fall until nightfall.

Ava could see how exhausted Catherine had become from all of the drama of the last few days, and as Catherine laid her head on the pillow, she swept her hair away from her forehead in a gentle, soothing movement until she drifted off.

Once Catherine was asleep. Ava sat on the edge of the bed and wept silently.

For the time being, home was Maria's house. Catherine's mother's home was conveniently situated, only a few plots away from the D'Souza's. Sadly, now their house had been so severely damaged in the fire plans had been made to have it demolished. Nevertheless, Ava and Maria managed to retrieve a few items from

Agnes's room, though everything in Catherine's bedroom was burnt or covered in black soot.

They both stood in the doorway of Catherine's workroom. Silence fell upon them, and they both felt sad at losing a life. Ava had always had a deep distrust of William hence she had always felt protective over Catherine. Since meeting her as a small child, Ava had been in her life and watched her grow into a beautiful, kind woman. But now she felt utterly helpless and couldn't take away her pain.

William, in her opinion, had been a good-for-nothing chancer who didn't deserve her beautiful Catherine; even so, she wouldn't have wished this end for him – or anybody.

After standing there for only a few moments more, they walked down the marble staircase and left the house for the last time.

On hearing of the imminent demolition of the D'Souza's house, Suhani decided to go back and see if any of her possessions were retrievable.

Walking through the garden, she pushed the kitchen door open and went into her room. Luckily there was only slight smoke damage. Picking her bag up off the floor, she managed to pack a few items and then got ready to leave. She made her way back through the door into the garden, but something stopped her, a nagging feeling to go back to the workroom to say her last goodbye.

Once in there, she began to speak to William as if he could hear her, knowing his body was no longer there, but that perhaps his spirit still was.

'Why, William? Why did you go? We had so much to look forward to. I waited for you; I wore your favourite sari, you know – the red one – and Hlaing cooked your favourite meal. But you didn't come to me, William. I waited and waited for you, but you never came. I am so sorry, William; I didn't see you in here – if I had, I would have dragged you out instead of her, but I never saw you.'

Dropping to her knees, she cried, 'I didn't save you! I didn't save you, my darling, please forgive me!' Nobody heard her cries.

Catherine decided to take one last look at her once beautiful, happy home, although now it was merely a burnt-out pile of wood and stone with just a few reminders of its former glory. Climbing over the wood and tiles, she went up the stairs.

Ava and Catherine's mother had tried desperately to persuade her not to go back, but they didn't understand. As she walked up the once-grand stairs, she suddenly heard William's voice; turning around, she saw him rushing through the front door.

He's alive! she thought. William was there, in front of her. Had all of this just been a horrible nightmare?

'Look, Catherine!' he said excitedly. 'Look, this house is beautiful!' Pulling her close, he kissed her gently and whispered, 'This is our new home, Catherine, ours and the baby's,' and he placed a hand on Catherine's stomach. She blinked, reached out to touch him, to hold him, to breathe him in, just one more time, but he was gone.

Sitting down on a step, she looked at the shell of her beautiful home and heard Agnes's laughter, and smiled as she saw William spin her around as she clung round his neck. They had such a close relationship, and she loved her daddy so much; he was her world, but now he had left. Burying her head in her lap, Catherine sobbed deep sorrowful cries from her broken heart, stopping suddenly when she heard the sound of a woman's voice coming from an upstairs room. She wiped her tears and continued up the stairs to the landing. She stopped; it was Suhani. Stepping back, Catherine listened by the door, not wanting to startle her.

'William, if you can hear me, just know I will always love you, and I will never forget what we shared for all those six wonderful years. You will always be the love of my life.'

Catherine felt faint and held on to the wall for support.

Hearing the noise on the landing; Suhani rushed out and saw Catherine standing there. Worried that Catherine might have overheard her words, she quickly said, 'Mrs D'Souza, you shouldn't be here; it's not safe. How long have you been in the house?'

Catherine looked straight at her and replied calmly, 'Not long.'

'Please let me help you downstairs. Please be careful: it's very slippery. I gathered a few items from my room, just looking over the house last time. I heard it might be demolished? That is so sad — it was such a lovely home for you all.'

'Yes, it was, Suhani: a happy home.'

'I know this probably isn't the best time to ask, but I was wondering: now that you are living with your mother and Agnes, and it's such a big house for the three of you, would your mother employ me? It would be like old times, but without Mr D'Souza.'

'I don't think so, but I will do my utmost to find you an employer that will suit you.'

'Oh, that is very kind of you. I will miss you all.'

'I am sure you will. Please come over to my mother's house this afternoon. I should have some news for you by then. I do understand your situation; we can't have you out on the streets now, can we?'

Catherine left the house for the final time and did not look back.

It took Catherine several more days to find the strength to face people before she felt able to take the short walk to the Carters' house. Several neighbours stopped her on the way, saying:

'I am so sorry to hear about your husband, Mrs D'Souza.'

'William was a good man; he will be missed.'

'If there is anything we can do, please don't hesitate to ask. You must be devastated, Mrs D'Souza.'

Thanking them for their kind words, she was relieved to soon be knocking on the Carters' door.

Suhani's mother, Daya, answered the door and led her into the drawing room. After asking to speak to Mrs Carter, Catherine knew Daya understood, although she couldn't speak much English. Daya took Catherine's hand and held it close to her heart and, before they reached the room, she said in broken English, 'Mr D'Souza, sorry,' squeezing Catherine's hand.

Knowing what Daya meant, Catherine bent down and hugged her; they had shared the birth of Agnes, and she would always be indebted to her. There was mutual respect between the two of them and they did not need words. Daya went to fetch tea whilst Catherine waited patiently in the drawing room. A shrill voice broke the quiet of the room.

'Catherine,' Mrs Carter called, rushing into the room. 'I am so sorry, I wasn't expecting a visit; I was in the garden.'

'I am sorry, I don't want to keep you,' Catherine said apologetically.

'Not at all, my dear; please sit down.'

'I can't stop long ...'

'Goodness me, you look like you've just seen a ghost ...' Mrs Carter stopped, realising what she had said. 'Oh, my dear, I do apologise, the wrong turn of phrase – please forgive me.' Ushering Catherine to sit down, she removed her sun hat and gardening gloves, then rang a small bell by her chair.

Daya entered the room. 'Daya, tea for Mrs D'Souza and myself.'

'Yes, Memsaab,' Daya replied, and she went back into the kitchen.

'Please excuse the staff. She isn't getting any younger; it might take a little while for your tea.'

'That is fine. I know Daya: she is the mother of Suhani, my servant.'

'Of course ... what is to become of young Suhani? I hear she is a very competent servant girl.'

'Oh yes, she has many skills. That is the reason for my visit – knowing that my circumstances have changed and I am now living with my mother, I wondered if you needed any more staff?'

'My dear girl, how rude of me; I haven't even passed on our deepest condolences to you and your family on the unfortunate loss of your husband. It must have been such a shock for you. He was such a lovely man. I always said to Mr Carter, 'you will not find a happier family than the D'Souzas on this side of Rangoon.'

Catherine remained calm. After all, Mrs Carter didn't know what a lying, cheating philanderer William had been. 'That's very kind of you to say, Mrs Carter,' she replied, just as Daya carried in the tray of tea. She placed it carefully on the small table between them, nodded to Catherine and left. 'We will not require her services, and I have promised to find an appropriate employer as soon as possible.

'Well, Daya could do with the help, and as they are mother and daughter, I am sure we can come to some arrangements financially for them.

'We have had a few young girls here; Mr Carter seems to take a natural shine to them, though he can be a real taskmaster with them. In the end, a bit like young foals, he soon has them eating out of his hand. He has a natural way with them – funnily enough, he doesn't seem to have the same patience with the older ones. But, yes, I am sure Suhani will fit in well, especially under Mr Carter's guidance.'

'That sounds perfect for her. My aim was for her to be employed where she could show her new employer all the skills that she has learned under Mr D'Souza's guidance for the past six years. He too enjoyed teaching her to be a good servant girl.' Catherine sipped her tea, happy at the thought of Suhani under the strict guidance of Mr Carter. 'That is so kind of you. I can't wait to inform her of her new employers.'

Once Catherine had finished her tea, she made her excuses and left the house, walking quickly back to her mother's. As she arrived, Suhani was waiting by the door, eager for employment news.

'Good afternoon, Mrs D'Souza,' she said.

'Good afternoon, Suhani. I have spoken to a lovely couple who are very happy to take you on.'

'Goodness, thank you so much, Mrs D'Souza, you are very kind, thank you,' Suhani said, excited at the prospect of a new employer.

'Please don't thank me, it's the very least I could do for you after all the years of hard work and loyal service you have given to me … and of course to *Mr* D'Souza, who enjoyed the time you shared with him and the family.'

Suhani noticed a sudden change in Catherine's tone of voice and this made her feel uncomfortable.

'Yes, I have managed to secure a position for you at The Carters' house. I am sure you will be thrilled working for them – and especially with Mr Carter, although I hear he is pretty strict with the new girls, he is ready to welcome you with open arms.

Your mother will be thrilled to have you with her too, but I think you might have to share a room with her. Not all bad though, you can keep her company in the evenings; now won't that be lovely for you, Suhani?'

Suhani stood there in silence. If only she were allowed to say no, but as usual, her destiny was in the hands of others.

Being a young Indian girl with no home, no money and only her charms as currency, she did what she had to do to survive; this life hadn't given her a choice. Once a servant girl, always a servant girl. Men had used her for their own needs since she was a child. How stupid of her to believe William: he was just like all the rest.

'Thank you, Mrs D'Souza, I will take the job.' As she turned to leave, she said, 'You were the first employer that ever made me feel part of the family. I will never forget that, Mrs D'Souza, and I am sorry … how everything turned out.'

Catherine nodded, accepted her apology, knowing what she was trying to say without saying the words. Suhani gathered her items together and put them in her bag.

'Can you please say goodbye to Agnes for me?'

'I will,' replied Catherine.

Leaving the house, Suhani pulled the bag up onto her shoulder and headed down the road to her next home; she looked back at Mrs D'Souza, who was still watching her from the kitchen door.

Walking back into the kitchen, Catherine made tea, pulled a chair out from under the table, and slumped down.

Does Suhani deserve Mr Carter? Absolutely, but perhaps, she thought, *if I was in her shoes, I too might have looked for a way out of poverty?*

She felt a slight twinge of guilt, but it soon passed after picturing the two of them together behind her back. Suhani was a survivor and would soon be lining up her next hope for a better life.

Hearing small footsteps coming down the hallway, Catherine quickly gathered her thoughts and began to make a pot of tea.

'Mummy!' Agnes shouted, running in and hugging her around her waist.

'Hello Agnes.' Catherine bent down and kissed her daughter on the top of her head.

'Mummy, when is Daddy coming home? I miss him, and I wanted to tell him about the chickens.'

Trying to remain calm, Catherine replied, 'And what about the chickens, Agnes?'

Catherine had so much to think about that she had completely forgotten about the poor hens. Thankfully, Maria had arranged for a worker to start building a run in a small corner of her garden so they could transfer them over.

Agnes had insisted that the hen house her daddy had built had to be moved to her garden, not forgetting their ladder. Maria had laughed to herself after Agnes said, 'How would they reach, Grandma? They can't fly very far; they are just chickens!'

Maria had held her granddaughter's hand as they went into the garden to fetch the ladder and, looking at her innocent face, tried hard to hold the tears back.

'Why are you so sad, Grandma? The chickens are ok.'

'Yes, my darling, they are all fine; it's just that the house looks so sad now, Agnes, that's all.'

Agnes looked over to her once beautiful home.

'Don't worry, Grandma, we can stay at your house now,' she said, and her little face lit up.

Agnes had settled well into Maria's house and loved being there.

'Mummy, when the workmen finish the new chicken run, can we tell Daddy? Can he come and see how happy Buttercup and the girls are in their new garden?'

Catherine looked over at her mother, and knew it was time to tell Agnes where her Daddy had gone. Reaching over, Maria took her daughter's hand; she knew how difficult this would be.

'Grandma is just going to see how your lovely chickens are, Agnes. Now come and sit down next to Mummy – she wants to have a little talk with you.'

Agnes ran and fetched a jar of kulkuls from the pantry and, placing it on the table, pulled up a chair and sat patiently waiting for Grandma to bring her milk. Dipping kulkuls into milk was one of Agnes's favourite treats.

Looking across at her mother, she said, 'You look such a sad mummy. Have you been crying?'

'Oh, I must have something in my eyes, dust or something.'

She could feel the anxiety rising from the pit of her stomach, only to be released by uttering certain words.

Those exact words that had given her sleepless nights, those exact words she had spoken out loud in her head a million times.

But there was no easy way of telling her daughter without breaking her heart. Leaning across the table, Catherine took her little hand and said, 'Agnes, I need you to be a courageous girl for me. Do you think you can do that?'

'Of course, Mummy, Grandma says I am getting a big girl and said I was a brave girl when all my toys went black and I didn't cry.'

'You are a courageous little girl indeed, Agnes.' Catherine's head was full of thoughts of William, but she continued, 'Mummy and Granny and you and Buttercup and all the chickens live here now, don't we?' Agnes nodded her head with a mouthful of kulkuls.

Catherine waited for her to finish, looking at her sweet little face with those beautiful brown eyes. She was the image of her father. 'Agnes, do you remember when we lived at our house, and you found Dolly in the yard, and she wasn't moving?'

'Yes,' Agnes replied. 'Daddy said it was a fox.'

'Yes, it was a very naughty fox. And do you remember where Dolly had gone?'

Agnes thought hard for a moment before replying. 'Daddy said to look up in the sky because she had gone to heaven in the clouds.'

'That's right, Agnes, and now …' Catherine paused, struggling to find the words, '… and now, your daddy has gone to heaven,' she said, fighting back the tears.

Agnes looked up. 'Is Daddy coming back, Mummy, back from heaven? Can I see him? I miss him.'

'I am sorry, Agnes, my darling, but Daddy won't be coming back.'

'Will he be looking after Dolly and Grumps?'

'Absolutely, yes he will be, and he will take great care of them both.'

'OK, Mummy, can I go to my room now?'

Catherine knelt beside her and held her close; she could feel her little chest rising and falling with quiet sobs. Then, taking her by the hand, she walked her to her room, where Agnes climbed onto her little bed.

'I am going to tell Teddy where Daddy has gone.' Taking the toy from her pillow, she pressed it close to her face and held it tight.

'All right, I will go and prepare supper, and when you have told all your toys, come and eat.'

Kissing Agnes gently on the forehead, Catherine left and pulled the door ajar. Watching Agnes line all her toys up on the end of her bed, she could hear her explaining to them that her Daddy was now in the clouds. Catherine watched through the gap in the door, with tears streaming down her face.

'Why, William? You had it all, everything you dreamed of and more – and now look. Look at our daughter breaking her little heart!'

Walking back to the kitchen, she began to think how well Agnes had taken the news, and could hear William's words: 'It is what it is.'

21

Her Father's Eyes

The day of William's funeral had arrived.

Catherine woke to the sun streaming through the shutters of her window. She put on the silk dressing gown her mother had lent her last night and went down to the kitchen and through to the garden. She sat down on the wicker chair and gazed out over the garden, though her mind was elsewhere, not seeing the plants or the trees. She could feel the fresh morning breeze move slowly over her skin, and she closed her eyes. The coolness of its touch was reminiscent of William's fingers gently running over her skin, his warm lips kissing her arm, neck and, lastly, her mouth. Her thoughts had left her with only one vision, and that was of William.

All night she had dreamt of being in his arms, with him kissing her, and making love to her at Halpin Road.

They had been so happy there, but everything had changed once they had moved to the new house. *He* had changed. She had loved him so completely, but he had betrayed her and taken her love for granted. Had he ever loved her, or was their marriage built on a pack of lies and deception?

How could she be the grieving widow of a husband she didn't know? How would she get through today?

It was time to get ready; Maria had left her a set of clothes to change into and they were hanging on the back of her bedroom door. Agnes had insisted on coming too, although Catherine was worried it might be too much for her.

Nobody spoke much once breakfast was over – too many thoughts and apprehensions filled their heads. Once they had all dressed, Maria helped Agnes with her little black veil, then she turned to her daughter and placed her hand on Catherine's. 'The hearse is outside; I will take Agnes and wait for you. Take your time and come out when you're ready.'

Catherine stood silent in the safety of the kitchen and closed her eyes. She could picture the three of them in the garden, laughing and playing ball with Agnes; the tears began to stream down her face. 'How could you, William? You have broken my heart.'

But she had to be strong for Agnes. Wiping her tears, she pulled down her veil to cover her face, picked up her black gloves from the table and walked out onto the street.

As she stepped out, she could see all her neighbours standing at their gates, heads bowed. Looking across the road from the house, a crowd of at least a hundred men stood in silence. Indians, Burmese, Chinese port workers and port staff led by Mr Simmons had gathered to see him off. Shocked by the enormous numbers that wanted to pay their respects, Catherine was approached by William's boss, Lucas, offering his deepest condolences.

She thanked him and soon found herself in front of a crowd of people along the whole street and beyond.

Four black horses with high plumes of ostrich feathers on each headgear stood in front of her, shuffling, eager to move. Glancing briefly at the glass hearse, unable to comprehend that William was in there, she walked to the back where Maria joined her. Taking Agnes's little hand in hers, they followed the slow procession to the church and flowers were thrown as they passed the neighbours houses. Agnes bent down and picked up a white rose and held it tight.

Arriving at St Mary's Cathedral, the pallbearers removed the coffin from the hearse, lifted it onto their shoulders and walked into the cathedral. Catherine was in a daze.

Walking down the central aisle reminded her of their wedding day. She was wearing her beautiful wedding dress and was on her father's arm. She could see William waiting anxiously at the altar; he turned and smiled at her.

Ushered into the front pew, Catherine, Maria and Agnes sat down, shortly joined by Ava. Catherine could hear the hymns in the background and see the priest saying Mass; she followed its direction purely through habit, but couldn't hear the words. Suddenly she was jolted from her daze, hearing her name called. 'Catherine, Catherine: it's time for you to say a few words.' Catherine looked blankly at Ava,

'Would you rather I did it, if you don't feel up to it?'

'No, no, thank you,' Catherine said, taking a piece of paper from her handbag and making her way along the pew. She was met by Father Doyle, who took her hand and led her to the pulpit. Placing her piece of paper down and smoothing it out, she looked up. To her amazement, the church was packed, not a single pew was empty, and people were standing at the back. Looking back at the front bench, she could see little Agnes holding her teddy and Grandma's hand.

She began:

'William Arthur D'Souza, many of you might know him by many other pet names, work names, but to me, he was simply my William. He was my husband, and father to our only child, Agnes. He was born in Rangoon and lived with his parents, Emilio and Marta, unfortunately they passed away several years ago, but I know how proud they would have been of William.

Everyone he met loved him, and his charisma and charm soon captured everyone's hearts. Determined that his great break would come one day, he worked hard and long hours to provide for his family.

I remember the day Agnes arrived; I had never seen him so happy. He had tears in his eyes and vowed he would be the best father he could be – and he was.'

She paused, her eyes filled with tears, and she could no longer see the words. Then, grabbing the paper from the pulpit and unable to hold back her tears, she quickly walked back to Maria. Once father Doyle had finished saying Mass, the congregation stood up and made their way out of the church. Catherine was first to pass the coffin.

'Goodbye, William, you were all I ever needed.' She touched the coffin gently as she walked out of the church.

The four pallbearers walked towards the coffin, lifted it onto their shoulders and left the church for the graveside. The crowd parted to make room for them to walk behind the Rite of Committal. The grave had been dug, and as they got closer, Agnes looked worried and held her mummy's hand tight. Standing close to the edge, the men laid the coffin onto the wooden struts.

As they lowered the coffin into the ground, Father Doyle began his prayer: '*In sure and certain hope of the resurrection to eternal life through our Lord Jesus Christ ...*' His words began to fade into the ether, and all Catherine could hear was her beating heart getting louder and louder in her ears; she had a tightness in her chest, and her palms began to sweat. She watched the cloth slipping slowly through their hands and noticed the dappled sunlight seeping through the trees and the warm breeze on her face. Everything slowed down. Then, after a few moments, the priest's words became audible again: '*... and we commit William's body to the ground earth to earth, ashes to ashes, dust to dust.*'

Catherine was handed a bowl of earth, she took a small handful and let the soil slip through her fingers over the coffin. Agnes moved closer to the edge, still holding Catherine's hand and threw the rose into the grave. 'Bye-bye, Daddy,' she whispered.

Catherine couldn't bear it anymore and slumped to her knees; Ava grabbed her arm before she ended up in the grave with William. Catherine saw a white glow in the distance beyond the grave – it was William, and he was smiling at her. He held his hand out for her to take; she stretched to reach it, but he faded away and was gone. She called after him, but he didn't reply.

'Where am I?'

'You are at the church, Catherine; you fainted,' replied Ava, helping her up and leading her to the bench.

'It's still happening then? I thought it was all a bad dream,' Catherine cried.

'I am so sorry, Catherine.'

Everyone left the graveside, except for Catherine, who asked for a few minutes alone.

Maria took Agnes to see the rest of the family.

Sitting on the bench, Catherine felt numb. Was this really happening to her? She thought about the crowds outside the house; she knew William would have thought it to be quite marvellous for such a turn out for him. It was just a shame he wasn't here to see it. Eventually, standing up, she walked towards the church.

'How is she?' asked Ava to Maria.

'Not good, as her mother I could always make it right, but today it is out of my hands,' she said, reaching for her handkerchief.

'She needs a little time alone, I will keep an eye on her, I can see Agnes needs you.'

'Thank you, Ava, I honestly don't know how we would have got through this awful ordeal without you.' she said taking her hand, 'and I know Catherine feels the same.'

'It's the least I can do, you are family to me.' she replied hesitantly. Ava felt a tug at her heart as she spoke the words. She had to remain silent.

Maria went to rescue Mr Simmons from Agnes pulling him through the crowd of mourners and as she looked over to the churchyard's entrance saw the figure of a young woman and a small child near the gate. At first, she couldn't make out who it was but as they got closer she soon realised who they were. Her pace quickened as she reached them.

'Ava, Ava look what mummy brought me,' said the child, holding up a tiny doll.

Not wanting to ignore the child, Ava bent down and said, 'What a beautiful dolly, Hope', Turning to the girl's mother, she whispered, 'What on earth do you think you are doing here, Isobel? You know you cannot be associated with William, what were you thinking? You need to go right now before Catherine sees you.'

'Hello,' said a voice, Ava swung round to see Catherine standing behind her.

There was an awkward silence, only broken by Isobel's words. 'I am so sorry for your loss, Mrs D'Souza.'

Catherine didn't recognise the woman, but she thanked her anyway.

'Mummy!' Agnes called, running towards her. 'Mummy, Mr Simmons is going to take Grandma and me on a trip on one of Daddy's ships!'

'That will be good,' Catherine replied, looking at her daughter's sweet face. Agnes then began to talk to the small child who was standing behind the woman. 'Who are you talking to, Agnes? she asked as the children squealed with delight. 'What are you laughing at Agnes, what is so amusing,' she asked, curious at Agnes delight.

Agnes grabbed the child's hand and pulled her across to meet her mother.

Catherine froze at the sight of the small child and suddenly felt a new tightness in her chest. Struggling to catch her breath, she screamed, 'No, surely not, not today, not when I have just buried him!'

'Mummy, Mummy what's wrong? Mummy?' Agnes cried.

Hearing the commotion, Maria ran to Catherine's side. 'Whatever is the matter, Catherine?' she asked. Looking at her daughter's face, she followed her view and said, 'Oh my … no, please say it's not ...?' Her words stopped, as she looked at the child's mother and then the child in absolute disbelief.

Catherine, unable to control herself, lunged at Isobel. Ava tried holding her back, but it was too late and Isobel felt a hard forceful slap across her face.

She shouldn't have gone to the funeral, she knew that, but she needed to say goodbye to William. She cried, 'I am so sorry, Ava, truly I am,' the tears streaming down her face. 'Hope needed to say goodbye.' Grabbing her daughter's hand, Isobel ran out of the churchyard.

Catherine, shaking with rage, walked up to the graveside, looked down at the coffin and said, 'How could you! I gave myself to you completely; my whole life revolved around you. Yet you were sleeping with *her* all the time, and God knows who else. I loved you, and promised in front of God to obey you, and yet all the time …'

Now she had proof of her husband's deceit; she had never felt such hatred for him. This was the final humiliation he could have bestowed on her: his parting shot into the afterlife. This was a living nightmare – she could already feel everyone staring at her and whispering behind her back. Her friends and neighbours began to leave the churchyard.

Catherine turned her back on everyone, too ashamed and embarrassed by the whole scene. Once the other mourners had left, she needed to get out of there as fast as possible and she ran to her mother's house. She could see her neighbours standing by their gate. When they realised it was Catherine, they immediately stopped their gossip, but it was too late: she had already heard the worst.

'Of course it's his child,' one said.

'You only needed to look at her,' said the other.

'Oh yes, she definitely has her father's eyes.'